Show Me a Sign

Ann
Clare
LeZotte

SCHOLASTIC PRESS / NEW YORK

Library of Congress Cataloging-in-Publication Data available

ISBN 978-1-338-25581-2
10 9 8 7 6 5 4 3 2 1   20 21 22 23 24
Printed in the U.S.A.   23
First edition, March 2020

DEDICATED TO

THE MEMORY OF

MY BROTHER,

PETER GEORGE LE ZOTTE (1968–2016),

AND TO

THE FELLOW DREAMERS

AND ADVENTURERS

OF OUR YOUTH

The Deaf . . . are everywhere . . .

They existed before you spoke of them

and before you saw them.

⌐LAURENT CLERC,
DEAF FRENCHMAN, AND THE FIRST
DEAF TEACHER IN AMERICA

⌒PROLOGUE

If you are reading this, I suppose you want to know more about the terrible events of last year—which I almost didn't survive—and the community where I live.

Every small village must think itself perfectly unique. I now know there was not another like ours in America, in the Year of Our Lord, 1805. For those who take hearing and speaking for granted, our way of life may be hard to understand.

You may be fooled into believing that Chilmark, on Martha's Vineyard—an island south of Boston—is a fancy of my imagination. Or the lost paradise that the English captain who named the land after his daughter was seeking long ago.

I've tried to be true to every detail and do justice not only to my friends and family, but also to my ene- mies. It was the stranger invited to our shores who changed my view forever.

I warn you, there are accounts of great wickedness along with hope in these pages.

As for my mastery of the language, I will remind you that not every writer comes to English from the same direction.

My story is built not with brick and mortar, but by finding the right words and making events come to life. If it were a palace, it would have many windows and doors—to see your reflection, peer into, and walk through. I hope you will be brave enough to enter.

Mary Elizabeth Lambert

Part
One

Chapter One

I like to walk early in the morning, before I begin my chores, even in this crisp November weather. I use my birch stick to poke at curious things on the ground, like the tunnels made by moles. They go so deep, they churn up the sand below the soil.

When I leave home early enough, I can see bright flashes from the Gay Head Light in the distance. But today the sun is up.

I run my stick across the top of the mossy stone wall that frames the high road and watch the sea glitter behind gabled houses with sloping yards. Sea grass borders the sand, blowing lightly in the cool breeze. Blue crabs burrow into the mud near the shore, where they'll lay dormant for the winter.

On the beach, there's little left of the humpback whale that washed upon our shores four days ago, delivered by the Almighty.

My closest friend, Nancy Skiffe, and I discovered the whale while playing. It was already dead when we found it, but its smell was not yet putrid. Small sea-birds pecked at its carcass. Its sea-worn, mottled black skin was covered in humps and bumps. We were awe-struck by its massive bulk.

Nancy and I walked a large circle around it. I collected scallop shells, moon shells, and quahog shells and put them next to the whale, as a final offering from a human friend. Nancy took a recorder out of her cloak and played a song to guide the beast to its end.

When Nancy and I ran to get her father, my papa, and the other men, they came with spades, knives, rope, and wheelbarrows.

As they made plans to dispose of the whale, Papa, sensing my sadness, signed to me assuredly, "Not one piece shall go unused. Meat for the whole town, oil for our lamps, and baleen in the beast's mouth for brushes."

I couldn't watch as our treasure was flensed, cut, and taken away, piece by piece.

I stop and write *whale* in the sand with my stick. I love words, but they confound me too. The way my mind thinks is not just in signs or English words and sentences, but in images and a flow of feeling that I imagine resembles the music I've never heard.

I watch the tide leaping in and out.

I pass a stretch of high road that I have come to avoid. I circle around it as if it is hallowed ground and head back home. Leaves jump and twirl ahead of me; the wind beckons me toward a small graveyard. I choose to ignore its silent whispers.

Chapter Two

Great warmth and a savory smell emanate from our kitchen. A large, clean brick fireplace dominates the room, along with the kettle hanging from a trammel hook. I step through a beautiful slice of sunlight on the floor and touch my mother's back.

"Morning," she signs, one hand rounded like the sun, the other arm acting as the horizon it climbs.

"Morning. Cooking?" I ask, mimicking stirring a pot.

Mama signs, "For supper."

She points to the meat pie on the table. I helped her make it two days ago. Today is the last serving. She places the pitcher beside me on the table. I'm to fill it from a shallow well in our yard. "First pie eat."

Mama delicately wipes the back of her hand across her sweat-beaded forehead. Even with the dirt smudges, her face is beautiful, with cheeks reddened by the fire. Her black hair and blue eyes are like coal and sky. George had her coloring. Mama glances at his empty chair and blinks away unshed tears. Then she's back to work, with her spoon dipped in the large kettle.

I dutifully finish the last piece of meat pie and grab the pitcher. Mama taps me on the shoulder. I turn around to face her.

"Three," she signs, holding up as many fingers. I am to fill the pitcher three times, adding the water to the kettle two times. Always, the last pitcher is for cleaning up.

The task is easy enough. Papa dug a shallow well right next to our house, by the pear and apple trees. On an island, you can't dig a well too deeply unless you want to drink and cook with salt water.

Back in the kitchen, I rinse corn, beans, and squash from our garden. These foods grow plentifully in every season. The Wampanoag, the local Indians, call them "the three sisters." They work together to grow— corn provides height for the bean stalk, squash provides mulch, and the beans provide beneficial gasses to the soil.

There is much discord between the Wampanoag and us Vineyarders that I know worries Mama and Papa. Papa says that we both lay claim to the same tracts of land, and the Commonwealth of Massachusetts goes back and forth in its rulings. The Wampanoag believe land should be held collectively, rather than as personal property. How can that be?

Papa is sympathetic to the Wampanoag. Perhaps it's because he labors side by side with them on the farm. Mama socializes only with English women. She is glad early missionaries to the island succeeded in Christianizing so many Wampanoag. I was raised to accept her beliefs. But ever since George died too young and without just cause, I have begun to question everything.

When I'm done cooking, I'm supposed to wipe the table, but instead I watch Mama wash a dish and wonder at her contentment with her daily chores. She always does them meticulously and with great calm. The last time I stacked the plates, I chipped two of them. I prefer making up stories.

"I saw a lion on the beach today," I sign.

Mama wrinkles her brow as she carefully lays a pan of hot cranberry muffins on a trivet.

She shakes her head and signs, "You shouldn't tell tall tales."

"But it's true," I insist, tapping my index finger against my closed lips.

"Tell me," Mama signs. She takes off her apron and sits down at the wooden table Papa built.

I sweep my hair away from my eyes—it is important that my face shows, even though it is positively dull. I don't have Mama's and George's fine features. My thick hair, which Mama calls the color of sunlight, has cowlicks that don't curl as smartly as other girls' hair. It gives me lumpy braids, and I'm too young for a bun. I tuck it behind my ears, and it hangs to the middle of my chest.

I remain standing so I can express myself with my whole body, not just my hands.

"When the tide came roaring in today, I saw the lion."

Mama frowns. "There are no lions on Martha's Vineyard," she signs emphatically. "Ezra Brewer put those ideas in your head."

"No, it was Miss Hammond. I love her teachings.

She always shares fascinating stories from her brother-in-law who is a sailor. He claims he saw a mermaid once. And Miss Hammond says the lion is 'the king of the jungle.'"

"We have no jungles, Mary. No lions."

Mama's eyes are watery and her shoulders slump.

"The dark waves were so high, and the sea spray was white against them," I sign, my eyes and mouth wide open to show awe. "I stayed back. One wave got bigger and bigger, and it looked like a lion's head roaring before it crashed against the rocks."

"That is fanciful," Mama signs. "It's not true life."

"But it looked like a lion to me," I sign.

I see Mama sigh. She has never had time for fancies. Papa enjoys when I tell a tale, and George was always most excited by my whimsies. His amusement at my storytelling made me perform more energetically. I sometimes even teased a smile out of Mama.

Mama stands up and begins to remove the muffins from the pan. I help her, then wrap two in a cloth.

"Walk beach, give to Ezra Brewer," I sign.

Mama nods, but I can read a slight look of disapproval in her face. Ezra Brewer is not Mama's favorite inhabitant of our township, Chilmark. I'm not sure why she dislikes him. Papa enjoys his company and stories. I sometimes wonder if his farmer's heart longs for the excitement of the high seas.

"I promise I'll return later to help you," I sign, crossing my fingers behind my back.

As I walk out the door, I think I see Mama call out to me from the corner of my eye. George was hearing like Mama. I am deaf like Papa, and no manner of shouting will get our attention.

I confess I do not turn back.

Chapter Three

We live up-island. To get to Ezra Brewer's, I walk down the high road toward our pastures. I do not see Papa or our herding dog, Sam. They must be back at the barn.

Our sheep farm sits on rolling meadows bounded by stone walls. From the high road to the Atlantic Ocean beyond, Chilmark is a hilly place. I sign, "Good morrow, sheep." They barely look up.

Our grazing pastures are part of the much larger Allen farm. With permission from the colonial government, the local sachem sold it to them in 1762. The Allens have rented the land to the Lamberts for generations.

I pass the timber-framed barn that Papa's father built. It has large tubs for sheep dipping and space for sheep shearing. In two small, adjacent buildings there is a very old corncrib for storing dried ears of corn, and a stone peat house, where rotting vegetation for conditioning the land is stored.

When I reach the hallowed ground on the high road, memories come rolling in like dark clouds.

My brother, George, and I are in the road. We are laughing. He is chasing me in circles, grabbing for a tool in my hand.

Clouds drift past the sun. I look up, shading my eyes with one hand when George slips the tool out from my other. I look directly into his face. He is smiling.

But then he pushes me hard. I am surprised by the force of his attack. I land facedown in the dirt with a thud. Then I see the flash of wheels.

They are fine wheels, black with gold trim. They spin fast. Toward George. Before he can do anything, one cracks, and George disappears underneath. I scream a scream I cannot hear.

I look up to see the horse's wild eyes. Even with the bit in its mouth, it seems to be squealing. It bridles, spooked. Where's George?

The horse cart swerves and comes to a halt, and that's when I see him. I scramble to my brother.

The driver hops off his seat and runs to George.

George's eyes are open. His lips smeared with blood. His chest still.

15

When I feel a hand on my shoulder, I shake it free. I look up into the face of Jeremiah Skiffe, Nancy's uncle. He seems twice the size of an ordinary man. He stares at George. He doesn't move. Was it his cart?

I stagger to my feet and stumble toward our house. My ankle stings; it twisted when George pushed me out of the way.

Mama is running from the house toward me. Did she hear my scream? Did she see? I collapse into her arms. "George" is all I sign. I don't tell her how we came to be in the road.

A hired laborer must have alerted Papa to the commotion and the yelling because I see him running to the high road.

Jeremiah Skiffe remains crouched by George's body but then stands to face Papa. He signs awkwardly. I cannot read his gestures. Papa makes no sign to him.

I watch Papa gather George in his arms. He slips in the mud as he carries him to the barn. Jeremiah Skiffe follows, attempting to assist in some way.

Mama lets go of me and runs to catch up with them. She sways as she touches her son. When Jeremiah Skiffe

gently steadies her by grasping her shoulder, she turns and
beats on his chest.

I pinch my arm to return to the present moment.
That was eight months ago, at the beginning of spring-
time. But inside me, it feels like fresh dew.

I turn my attention to the Hillman house. In
spring and summer, their yard is full of greensward,
and their fence and arched trellises disappear beneath
roses of every color and scent. Now all that richness is
covered with frost.

I go to school with the Hillmans' youngest
daughter, Sarah. I can't say that we are compatible. She
cares too much for appearances and wants other girls
to follow behind her. She doesn't mind that we don't
attend school year-round or study as many subjects as
the boys do. But I chafe at the unfairness. Though I
like our moving school that is situated in different
towns for different seasons, I wish I could attend
Edgartown Academy, where George boarded for weeks
at a time. He learned Latin and was preparing to enter
college. I wish I could bring home armfuls of books
and pore over them for the secrets they unlock.

Miss Hammond makes up for some of the unfairness by being such a wonderful teacher. Matthew Pye is courting her. I pass his blacksmith's forge; its soft-coal fire smoke fills my nostrils. I can feel the sound of the hammer on the anvil ring out through the air. I secretly hope Miss Hammond and Matthew Pye don't marry so she'll stay on as my teacher.

A little farther on, I spot Isaiah Butler standing atop the stone wall, holding his spyglass. When you look through the smaller end, you can see great distances magnified in the larger end. I have borrowed Papa's to watch for whales and to stargaze.

"Who?" I sign, curious who he is watching.

"John Skiffe," he spells with his fingers. Mr. Butler is a short, rotund man who is known to engage in gossip.

It is common practice for Vineyarders to use a spyglass to converse with neighbors whose houses are far apart. If they are hearing, signals are sent by blowing a large horn. Then both parties take up their spyglasses to read each other's signs. If the other party is deaf, like Mr. Skiffe, they choose a time.

"Did you know?" he signs to me. "A young scientist is coming to town! He stopped at Edgartown Harbor first. Look out for his schooner on the beach, the SS *Defiance*."

I have never met a scientist. Very few people stop at the Vineyard for anything more than trading.

"Why is he coming?" I ask.

"That I don't know," signs Mr. Butler. "Just that he's a friend of Reverend Lee coming to work on our island."

"Thank you for telling me," I sign, eager to tell Ezra Brewer. "Good day."

How exciting to have a stranger in our midst!

As a rule, our small island community does not take kindly to strangers. When they have docked down-island at Edgartown Harbor to bring us provisions and trade for our whale oil and wool, that's one thing. But unless they have a relative on the island, or a resident to sponsor or introduce them, strangers are met with suspicion.

While I walk, I make up a story to please myself. It's something I've done for as long as I can remember.

If I'm restless in bed, it helps me fall asleep. If I'm bored, it entertains me. Sometimes it helps me make sense of things that lack sense.

Miss Hammond says I have a vivid imagination and that I can tell the truth from lies. She says that I'm a natural storyteller. I hope to become a schoolteacher like her one day. Then I would have my own collection of books, and I wouldn't have to justify the urge to read and write rather than cook and clean.

I must look funny, walking along signing to no one in particular. Mama tells me it is no different from hearing people who talk to themselves.

I imagine a girl assisting a scientist with his great discovery. They are looking for a fresh spring. Not just any spring. This one contains sparkling water, and if you drink it, it makes you live forever. There is more than one map to the source. They search high and low, sometimes retracing their steps. They climb mountains and descend into valleys under the setting sun.

Finally, they discover the well. The scientist falls to the ground to drink from it before he even collects a sample. But the girl is unsure if she should drink it. Would she want to outlive all her loved ones?

My story trails off as I near my destination. I am conscious of a person who lurks in my shadow, just out of view.

Chapter Four

Ezra Brewer lives at the top of the beach. His one-story, pine frame house has a big brick chimney and scattered lobster traps lying about. He doesn't cultivate a garden, or own animals, aside from a one-eyed black cat named Smithy.

Even at his advanced age, Ezra Brewer is a seaman, with a stiffness in his joints and the breath of sea air in his lungs. He has a storied history of navigating his old cutter, the SS *Black Dog*, to Boston and beyond. He has sailed in nor'easters and never lost a man. And he can still cast a single fishing line and get the best catch of the day.

He sees me coming and waves his hand over his head. As usual, he is sitting on an old wicker chair on the porch.

For all the years I've known him, I have rarely been invited inside his home. Mama says he doesn't clean his house or person, and "cleanliness is next to godliness." I say it is just that Ezra Brewer has never taken a wife to fix up a proper home for him.

In the wake of my brother's death, his rather un-civilized way of living doesn't seem so unpleasant. It might be easier to be a hermit who lives on the beach than to endure the quiet sorrow in our home.

As I approach, I see he is wearing the same clothes he always wears no matter the season, a worn linen shirt, a blue wool waistcoat, broadcloth trousers, red wool socks, a knit Monmouth cap, and an old sealskin coat. His eyes are the darkest blue I've ever seen. His long gray hair hangs over his ear-lobes, which are pierced, though I never see him wear earrings.

I make a sour face when I see the bottle of rum he cradles in his lap. Mama is an abstainer. She does not allow alcohol in our house for pleasure drinking. We use it only for cooking and for medicine during times of illness. I recently learned from Miss Hammond that many find it healthier to drink ale than water. Do I dare to challenge Mama?

"Don't be judging me, missy," Ezra Brewer scolds. "Ye have not walked in my shoes."

I know he is right. Reverend Lee always teaches us to sympathize rather than to judge our neighbors. I hand Ezra Brewer the muffins, smile, and hold up my fingers to sign. "I'm sympathizing."

He throws back his head, and the power of his laughter shakes us both. Then he gulps down the muffins, looking satisfied. He hands me the cloth and lets Smithy lick his fingers.

To change the subject, I sign, "Mr. Butler says a young scientist is coming to Chilmark. A guest of Reverend Lee's. I wonder what research he plans to do in our town."

"I'll abide research," he signs. "So long as he doesn't try to take advantage of townsfolk."

"Why would he do that?" I ask.

"Outsiders," he signs. "Never give them credence at first. Only welcome them after they've proved themselves trustworthy."

"That's not very friendly," I sign.

"Never said I was," he signs.

I shake my head and sign, "Tell me the story of where our people come from."

"I've only told you two dozen times before," he signs. He puts the cork back in the bottle and sets it down beside his chair. Smithy takes her place in his lap.

24

"The story . . . ," he muses.

"Tell me why some of us are deaf and others are hearing," I prompt him.

"You know the answer to that, girlie," he signs. "Nobody knows."

"But why not? There have been deaf people, like you and me and Papa, since we came to the island."

"Aye, Mary, that's a fact," he signs.

Ezra Brewer says "aye" by jerking his head forward and wiggling the fingers on his left hand. Even though his hands are old and gnarled, he signs with great skill.

He works his jaw. He has a habit of moving his mouth for a bit before he signs a story. I think this comes from watching hearing people speak. I sometimes do it too.

Ezra Brewer begins, "There is a region in Kent, England, where many people are born deaf. It is called the Weald."

I interrupt. "That's a funny name."

Ezra Brewer gives me a look that could sink me to the bottom of the ocean. I think he is going to scold me, but he opens and closes his hands like he's gathering words out of the air.

"Aye," he signs, "Weald means 'woodlands.' It is a harsh place to live with its thick forest and tall cliffs made from limestone, so people decided to take a voyage and make new lives in the colonies. The deafness came with them."

"But why did it come with them?" I ask.

"I told you," he signs. "Nobody knows for sure. But if you ask me, our deafness must be caused by something in the blood."

"How can that be?" I ask. "Mama is hearing, George was hearing, and Papa and I are deaf. We have the same blood." Bloodlines are important to English settlers on the island. They tell us who we are and where we came from.

Ezra Brewer folds his arms across his chest, sniffs the air, and refuses to look at me. I've interrupted his storytelling too many times.

I untie my hat and dangle a ribbon in front of Smithy, who bats at it.

This must make Ezra Brewer feel charitable because he starts signing again. I try my best to keep quiet.

Even though my parents know our early history,

they are reluctant to talk about it. "A bird flies forward," Mama always says. Past, present, and future all seem mixed together in Ezra Brewer's mind.

He looks at me and makes words with his fingers as quickly as I can read them.

"Your great-great-grandfather Jonathan Lambert," he signs, "was the first recorded deaf person to settle on the island. He arrived in 1692, using sign language from England."

I smile. "But the sign language has changed since those days," I add, interrupting once again.

Ezra Brewer signs, "The language people speak on the island is not the King's English anymore. You are right. We have our own rules, signs for most words, and we can finger-spell the alphabet with both hands. Facial expressions and body language are as important as making the correct hand signs, while kinship makes it possible to understand each other with one or two signs or a look." He gives me a sidelong glance, which I know means I best stop interrupting.

He continues signing. "Jonathan Lambert was a good carpenter and farmer. In 1694, he bought a piece of land from Sachem Josias Wompatuck for seven pounds. I suspect ol' Jonathan got the better end of that deal. Today the place is still called Lambert's Cove. It's over by Christiantown. You've been there."

I nod my head and right fist simultaneously. Someone else is watching Ezra Brewer recount our history. I catch a glimpse of the shadow peeking around his house.

"He married a hearing woman. They had seven children, including your great-grandfather Edward. Each married into families who came to the island from the Weald too and gave birth to deaf and hearing children. Your ancestors. Jonathan Lambert died at eighty years old, leaving a large estate and a good reputation."

I smile. I like to hear that story.

"Aye," Ezra Brewer signs, reading my face. "You should be proud to be his kin."

"You never tell me about your kin," I sign.

A strange look passes over Ezra Brewer's face. He picks up the bottle and removes the cork. He has said all he is going to say for now. I have suspected for some time that he keeps a secret. I've asked Papa, but he won't tell me. I think it has something to do with Ezra Brewer's activities during the War for Independence.

I stand up, bring the open palm of my right hand down from my chin, and sign, "Thank you."

Ezra Brewer winks and takes a swig from his bottle.

I start to follow the high road back home.

The shadow also returns. I am not afraid. I know just who my tracker is.

Chapter Five

While I'm walking back along the high road, I think about what it must have been like when my great-great-grandfather Jonathan Lambert first came to the island. How did he communicate with other English settlers and the Wampanoag? What would it be like if the world were suddenly turned around, and everyone spoke but didn't sign?

The shadow grows closer. Because I don't hear, I rely heavily on my sight. Small details rarely escape my view. When I look back, Nancy ducks behind a tree, her arms held stiffly at her sides.

She is also eleven years, a thickset girl, with black curls pulled straight, lively brown eyes, and a sharp, boisterous nature. She lives off the high road too, a long walk uphill from our house. A walk so familiar to me I could take it in the dark. We have been best friends for as long as I can remember.

I see her crouch by a stone wall. I stop to remove a pebble from my shoe.

"Boo!" Nancy signs, opening her clasped hands in my face, as she jumps from a hedgerow right into my path.

When I don't scream or start, Nancy frowns and hits me playfully with a weed she pulls from the ground.

"Which spy are you today?" I sign.

"Miss Jenny," she spells with her fingers. "Do you know who she is?"

I make the letter O with both my hands to indicate I have no idea.

Nancy signs, "She was a British loyalist. She didn't want our country to be free from England, so she spied on the French troops who fought on our side and reported their activities to the British headquarters in New York City."

Nancy stops walking.

"Uncle Jeremiah says Miss Jenny was barely a mature woman, but she was very daring. When she was brought before General Washington for questioning, they cut off her hair . . ." Nancy flings off her hat and mobcap and pretends to cut her hair with imaginary scissors.

It's hard for me not to think of the accident when

31

Nancy mentions her uncle. Of course, it's not Nancy's fault that Jeremiah Skiffe killed George. We should not have been playing in the high road.

To make it worse, Nancy's father would not let the town council or Reverend Lee speak to Jeremiah before he fled the island to his estate near Boston. I wish they had both treated Papa and Mama more respectfully.

Their behavior reminds me of my own sins and that I too am keeping the whole truth about George from Mama and Papa.

"It was a sign of public shame," Nancy continues. "Hard as they tried to persuade her, Miss Jenny wouldn't confess."

Nancy raises the palm of her hand in front of her mouth and shakes her head defiantly to demonstrate Miss Jenny's refusal.

I remind her, "Miss Jenny was a traitor."

Nancy shrugs and repeatedly places the palm of one hand over the other. It's sign language for "nevertheless."

Suddenly, Nancy pulls me down behind the stone wall. She beckons for me to peek over the other side without being seen.

Reverend Lee is walking up from the beach with a

young man. It must be the scientist! I try to explain this to Nancy, but she hushes my hands.

I notice that Reverend Lee carries a carpetbag and the young man a black satchel. Does he intend to stay on for a while?

When they pass near us, I am struck by the stranger's resemblance to my brother. I must gasp, because Nancy places her hand over my mouth. I lick it to make her let go. She wipes it on her skirt.

I am uncomfortable squatting in the dirt. Once the men pass and have covered some ground, I stand up and dust off my clothes.

"One day," Nancy signs, "you'll see the use in my expert spying techniques."

I kick a stone to her. She kicks it back as we move up the road. Nancy was born hearing, but her parents, John and Laura Skiffe, are deaf. I've noticed that Nancy signs more than she speaks.

"I wish Ezra Brewer told a ghost story today," she signs. If there's one thing Nancy likes better than spy stories, it is ghost stories. Sadly, her mother forbids her from going to Ezra Brewer's. Like Mama, Mrs. Skiffe does not approve of him.

"That wicked old man with his bad luck cat," Nancy signs, and skips in circles around me, making the sign for "haunt" in the air.

"Stop!" I sign. "Don't be morbid. Remember George." Because he died so suddenly, I worry that his spirit is not at rest.

We both lower our hands and stop signing for a moment.

"I never told you this," she signs, "but the night Grandmother Edith died in her sleep, she appeared at the foot of my bed. She looked transparent as a veil. I wasn't shocked when she told me she felt cold as the grave, but she was quite surprised to be dead, even though she had a long illness."

I search Nancy for a twinkle in her eye, but she is not teasing me.

"Grandmother Edith was concerned about her teapot," Nancy continues. "It is a silver heirloom and quite valuable. She didn't want Mother to sell it. She told me I must find it under her bureau, polish it till I could see my reflection, and hide it in a safe place. She wanted me to use it when I marry and have my own home."

"Did you do it?" I ask, a chill running up my spine.

"It was exactly where she said it would be. I did as she said, and her specter never interrupted my sleep again."

"Where did you hide the teapot?" I ask.

"Oh," Nancy signs, with a wicked grin, "I don't think Grandmother Edith would like me telling you that."

I am stunned.

"I have an idea," Nancy signs. "But I am not sure you are going to like it."

"What?" I weakly sign.

"Maybe," she signs, "we can have a dance for the dead."

"That's blasphemy," I sign.

"You sound like your mother," Nancy signs, with a discernible frown. "No one would know. Since you did not attend George's funeral, this could be our own last rites for him, to lay him to rest."

A picture flashes through my mind: George wrapped in his death shroud. The day of his funeral, I had a high fever and was bedridden. I saw him only briefly from my upstairs window as Papa and Mama drove him in our cart to the churchyard.

Nancy signs, "We could wear winding shrouds and run through the woods near the old salt marsh."

I like the notion of honoring George. Could I really lull his uneasy spirit to rest? Could I commune with him, one last time, as Nancy did with her grandmother? Could I apologize for luring him into the road and ask forgiveness?

Surely Mama would scold me harshly if she knew. But Nancy said that it will be only us. I look at my friend's hopeful face. What would George do?

I am uncertain, but I sign, "Yes."

"Truly?" Nancy asks excitedly. She rubs her hands together, and for a moment, I doubt my choice.

"Tomorrow afternoon," I sign. If we wait too long, I might change my mind.

Nancy's face lights up like a sprite. "Say you are coming to visit me but take a turn off the high road and follow Littlewoods Lane. I'll meet you between the woods and the old marsh. I've trod the path more than once. You'll have to chart a course to avoid danger."

"How will I do that?" I sign.

"Find George's map," she signs.

We walk as far as Papa's farm and step on the stone wall to reach the branches of a large apple tree. It isn't easy to climb in a gown and stockings, but we manage to settle in the crook of a large branch.

Nancy reaches into her cloak pocket and pulls out her small wooden recorder. She begins to play, then stops. "My father tells me he finds it rude when I play in front of him and Mother. Do you ever mind that I play music in front of you, even though you can't hear it?"

I shake my head.

Nancy's father, John Skiffe, drinks heavily and is often ill-humored. It's Nancy's uncle Jeremiah who encourages her interest in music, but he hasn't returned to the island since the accident.

Nancy closes her eyes while she places her fingers on the holes of the instrument and blows the air from her full cheeks. Reverend Lee says she can pick out any tune after she's heard it played once.

Watching her play, I am experiencing the music in my own way. The way I imagine birdsong when I see birds soaring in the sky.

Just as with my storytelling, I think Nancy's music

making shows what she feels inside. Sarah Hillman and the other girls we know are only concerned with learning to run a household. They assist their mothers sewing clothes and rearing their younger siblings. They view us as childish and impractical. Even if they are right, we prefer our fancies.

Nancy opens her eyes and rests the recorder on her lap. Then she stares into the distance.

I follow her line of vision across Papa's farm. Our sheep and Thomas Richards, one of Papa's two farm laborers, are walking slowly toward us. Thomas is a former slave with broad shoulders and a long stride. He is dressed in worn workman's clothes.

Nancy starts to climb quickly down the tree. I follow her. She would hate to be compared to her fussy, pious mother, but I have seen Mrs. Skiffe shrink back from freedmen as Nancy does now.

When she reaches the ground and smooths her gown, she can barely get out the signs for "remember tomorrow" before she starts back up the high road to her house.

Chapter Six

Thomas approaches the stone wall. Some sheep have strayed from the flock, so he herds them by bumping their rears with his knees. They are an unruly bunch. I climb over the wall and try to help steer them with my birch stick.

"Hello," I sign. He nods amiably in response. "How is Helen?" I ask after his wife. She works as a housemaid at Nancy's house. "I have not seen her lately at the Skiffes'."

"Her mother has been ill, Mary," he tells me, "and she has been walking back and forth from home to be with her." Helen is Wampanoag from Gay Head.

"Is Sally with her?" I ask.

Sally is their ten-year-old daughter who sometimes works with her mama or spends time with her papa at our farm. She is a lively girl, full of sweetness and laughter. I envy her deerskins and moccasins with fine beadwork, which look more comfortable than my stays and gowns. But Mama forbids me from wearing such clothing.

"She's around here somewhere," Thomas signs, waving his hand in every direction.

Thomas used to help only in the spring with the big sheep shearing. But with George gone, he stays on year-round now.

When Thomas was a slave, his last master granted his freedom. Mama is cordial to him in their brief inter-actions, when he carries wood or butchered meat to the kitchen door, but he isn't invited into our home. Neither is our other hired hand, an Irishman, Eamon Reilly.

In our town, the Irish are seen as inferior to the English but superior to freedmen. Papa pays those ideas no heed and stubbornly hires both when others will not. I used to be embarrassed when our neighbors commented on Papa's radical notions. But George's death has opened my eyes to new ways of thinking.

"Might I follow you for a few minutes?" I ask Thomas.

"I cannot stop my work," he reminds me, "but you are welcome to join me."

In the distance, I locate Sally leaning against the railing of the paddock where we keep Bayard, a brown colt who will take orders from no one since George died. Is she not afraid of the sleek, volatile beast?

Once the sheep are reunited in the pasture, we head for the barn. I notice that while Thomas is dressed in broadcloth and wool like Papa, he has a new pair of deerskin boots.

"Is it strange for you to live among the Wampanoag?" I ask.

"Not at all," Thomas signs. "Why would you ask that?"

"Because you are not Wampanoag and they live differently from us," I sign.

"There are differences between Chilmark and Aquinnah," Thomas signs. "But the Wampanoag are my people now."

"Why do you say Aquinnah instead of Gay Head?" I ask.

"For the same reason I say Noepe instead of Martha's Vineyard. All Wampanoag use the names of our ancestors to name our land," Thomas signs.

I remember Papa saying the Wampanoag don't want their land divided into private parcels under the control of settlers, and that Chilmark was once a sachemship, a common land of the Wampanoag. I wonder what it was like then. Maybe they think that by using their ancestor's names they can hold on to Wôpanâak, the Wampanoag language that has almost disappeared since we settled on the island.

"But they are not your ancestors." I make the sign for a tree with long branches to indicate ancestors.

Thomas is scouring a table in the barn where a lamb was butchered. He rings blood from a sea sponge into a wooden bucket.

"They are my ancestors, Mary," Thomas explains. "My place is with the Aquinnah Wampanoag Tribe."

"But you don't have Indian blood."

Thomas looks squarely at me while he dumps the water in a trough and puts down the bucket to sign. "The Wampanoag don't see it the same way," he explains. "It's not just about blood. My wife, daughter, and I belong in the town of Aquinnah. We share the same beliefs and customs. We participate in ceremonies to honor the Great Being Moshup. We work hard to sustain our small community."

That doesn't make sense to me. Some Indians have joined our society. They are our neighbors, but we are still different and separate.

"What about Sally?" I ask. "She is half Indian and

half black. Mama says that means she can't lay claim to Wampanoag land."

"My daughter will inherit her mother's lands. My history is also her legacy. A few in Aquinnah disapprove of my marriage to Helen, but Sally belongs fully to the Wampanoag Nation."

"But Mama is half French, which means I am a quarter French," I sign to Thomas.

He smiles without answering and goes back to work. I think he knows he set my mind spinning.

Outside, Sally has entered Bayard's paddock. She extends her hand to the agitated animal. He snorts and kicks up dust. Sally holds still. Bayard does not take the treat she offers. He rears up on his back legs. I hold my breath and count to twenty.

Sally calmly slips under the fence, throws the dried corncob in the pen, and watches him eat. I release the air trapped in my chest. How can she be so unafraid?

George was bold too. He could ride Bayard. And while he pitched hay or raked Bayard's stall with Thomas, George would ask for accounts of his bondage, which he sometimes shared with me. It gave me nightmares to imagine children sold away from their parents, parted forever.

I want to be brave like Sally and George. I tap Thomas's shoulder. "What was your life like before you came to the island?"

Thomas bends down and peers directly into my eyes. "When I was your age, I was a slave in the Colony of Maryland. I shall not recount to you the horrors of my passage to your country, nor the plantation life that shackled me and tore my family apart . . . ," he trails off, his signs seared in my mind.

I lower my eyes while he stands and takes up a rake to clear the barn floor of dirty hay.

Massachusetts abolished slavery within the state in 1783, before I was born, but still it is something the adults prefer not to discuss. There is one slave we honor, Sharper Michael, the only man who died on our shores during the War for Independence.

Reverend Lee, who once owned a slave, preaches against men being bought and sold as property. Grown folk say the past was different. But Reverend Lee says slavery is against God. The laws changed, and his heart must have too.

I raise my hand to get Thomas's attention.

"I'm sorry," I sign. I can find no better words.

"I'm sorry about your brother," he signs back. "The loss of a loved one is the hardest thing to bear."

He closes his fist on top of his heart, to demonstrate a pain I feel daily.

"I want to go back and change what happened," I sign.

"Many people would like to turn back time," Thomas signs. "We must move forward from where we stand. The sun rises every day, and time goes on." Thomas makes the sign for "conversation" and the sign for "work."

I have kept him long enough. He has a list of chores to do for Papa, and Mama is expecting me at home. Sally approaches and looks at me nervously, asking with her eyes if I have told her papa that she approached Bayard. I shake my head to assure her I have not. She smiles.

Looking up at the sun, I realize I've been gone for hours. I wave goodbye and trudge home.

I find the sitting room empty.

The smell of chicken soup and a wood fire wafts from the kitchen.

I can detect Mama's footsteps upstairs. When the house is alive with activity, I sense vibrations through the wooden floors. Otherwise the house feels silent.

Silence. I'm sure that many hearing people, especially those who don't know the deaf, imagine our lives are filled with silence. That's not true. If my mind and heart are full of energy and fun, and I'm looking ahead with excitement, I don't feel silent at all. I buzz like a bee in good times. Only in bad times, when I am numb and full of sadness, does everything turn silent. Like our house with just Mama and me in it.

I climb the stairs slowly. Mama must hear me, but she doesn't come out to welcome me home. I peek into the room. She is at her loom, her back to me. She has a skein of spun wool in her hand. Her head is bowed. Is she weaving or crying?

I go downstairs. George's bedroom is next to Mama and Papa's and adjacent to the kitchen. I haven't entered it since the accident. But I need to find the map to chart my course to the old marsh.

Chapter Seven

Everything is where George left it eight months ago. There isn't a trace of sand. Mama must dust his bedroom while I'm out.

I am nervous as a bag of cats standing here, as if I should have asked permission to enter a room so familiar to me. I have not come here to steal anything, only to retrieve what's mine.

The first object that catches my eye is the conch shell that George used as a paperweight. I pick it up and a memory floods back.

One August day when I was six years old, we swam for hours in the ocean with Papa. It was the day Papa taught me to float on my back. The water was warm on the surface and cold underneath. Then we combed the beach for shells. Most of them had been pecked at by hungry gulls. But George found the large pink one, perfectly intact.

Papa signed for George to hold it to his ear.

George did, and his face lit up.

"What do you hear?" Papa asked him.

"The ocean!" George signed, making rolling waves with his hands and arms.

Papa nodded.

"How do you know, Papa?" I signed.

"Mama and others have told me," he explained. "If you travel from the island," Papa told George, "take it with you. You'll always hear our ocean."

George smiled. Then something changed in his expression. Tears came to his eyes.

"What's wrong?" I asked him, not wanting the sunny day to be spoiled.

"You," he signed, pointing at me and Papa, "will never hear it."

"Fine," Papa signed, reassuring him.

Now I wonder if it was fine. Then I think of our history since Jonathan Lambert arrived. Papa was right. We are fine as we were made.

As I caress the shell, I wonder, Does it still make the sound of the ocean without George's ear to hear it, or is the sea magic gone?

I put down the shell and cross the room to the chest of drawers. Instead of the map, I find a small box with an owl pellet. We found two pellets at the base of an oak tree last year. I thought they were dung.

"Mary, look," George signed, holding them in his hand.

I took a closer look and noticed that the outside of the pellets was furry. I pet them gently, still a bit disgusted by their strong smell.

George laughed in his quick, relaxed way.

"Owls eat small prey and then regurgitate them," he signed, finger-spelling many of the words. He was never a natural signer.

When he made the sign for "vomit," I pulled my hand away. "Vile," I signed.

He laughed again and signaled for me to follow him back to our house, where he put the basin from his bedroom on the kitchen table and sent me out for fresh water.

When I returned, he filled the bowl and put in one owl pellet. The water quickly turned brown. I leaned in closely. Mama stopped what she was doing to come and see what we were up to.

George loosened the pellet gently, then laid a cloth on the table. He placed small white objects that emerged from the pellet on the cloth. They were thin and curved like small teeth. He set down more and arranged them. I couldn't figure out what he was doing, until he unearthed a very small skull. I watched with fascination as he assembled a mouse's skeleton! Mama clasped her hands together with delight, and George looked proud. Nature is infinitely mysterious. I wanted to understand how owls knew to create the pellets. I looked in George's schoolbooks for more details, but I could find none.

George's books! Could he have tucked the map inside for safekeeping?

On a small shelf beside his bed are books that were never returned to Parson Thaxton. It is not like Mama to keep someone else's property. Perhaps she couldn't bear to part with anything left in George's room and Papa paid to replace them.

I pick up a book of legends and flip through the pages. Nothing. Then a book of Latin grammar. Still nothing. When I open a book about local geography, the map falls out.

I unfold it and touch the lines. Lines that George

drew. My mind conjures up his warmth and light. I try to hold on to the moment, but it fades.

Nancy and I had wanted a map of Chilmark. Not the kind cartographers make, but a map with all the places that are important to us. George counted drawing among his many talents, so he made it for us. He even included figures of me and Nancy walking on the high road and Smithy down by the Atlantic Ocean.

I touch the homes of families and friends we frequently visit, Ezra Brewer's house, the Allen farm, select apple trees, Mr. Pye's shop bellowing smoke, and the field where Mr. Butler's oxen wandered when he left his gate open one night.

It is a map of memories.

George was always adding new touches. The most recent was Sarah Hillman running from the schoolyard to the fresh spring with angry hornets chasing her. George was working on Thomas carrying a bale of hay when the accident happened.

A salty tear drops onto the map and stains the ocean.

I look closely at the path Nancy instructed me to

follow tomorrow. It's somewhere I rarely venture. Littlewoods Lane can be treacherous. The tall marsh grass hides small sinkholes. George marked them with skulls and crossbones.

These details were not dramatic touches. We have great respect for the power of the old marsh, and its stories of animals and birds caught, unable to free themselves, until they sink and die.

When we were younger, a group of us went down to the marsh together. Billy Hillman, Sarah's cousin, believed it was a lake and decided to wade in. He quickly became stuck in the deep, thick mud.

"Don't move! Don't try to free yourself!" George called out and signed.

But Billy struggled and sank deeper.

At George's command, we formed a human chain. George was closest to Billy, and he held his hand while we all pulled so we wouldn't lose Billy and George. Billy lost only one shoe to the grimy pit.

The shoe is a landmark on George's map of memories.

We never told our parents that we had tested death and won.

I trace my route for tomorrow. I will keep to the right side of the lane and approach the marsh to the north of Mr. Pye's shop.

Vibrations through the floorboards shake me out of my reverie. I quickly put everything back where I found it and step into the kitchen.

Mama is standing by the table.

"Heard sounds," she signs, looking stricken.

"Sorry," I sign.

Mama returns to folding linens, and I have no choice but to finish my chores before supper.

I wipe the ornate cupboard that has been passed down in our family. I put the dishes and cups I washed on its shelves. I look at Mama with a smile, hoping she'll praise my delicate work, but she remains absorbed.

When I return to my dusting, my rag brushes a hanging teacup. It teeters on its hook, slips, and falls, shattering on the wooden floor. It must have made a loud, sharp sound because Mama spins around. I quickly assure her that I will clean up the broken pieces.

I watch her mouth move, her brow pulled down in a scowl. She is yelling at me, without signing, as she collects the pieces of the cup in her apron. I can see her lips flying as she stomps over to the basin and dumps the shards inside.

I want to put my hands over my ears to remind her that I cannot hear her scolding. But tears are stinging the backs of my eyes, threatening to spill over. I wipe my wrist against the corner of one irritably.

I am grateful when Papa comes in, breaking the tension by stomping his heavy boots. He warms his hands by the hearth and pours a cup of tea.

"Mary," he signs, brushing his right hand gently across his cheek. He has used that sign for me since I was born and he first stroked my face. Then he pats me on the top of the head, like I am still his little girl.

In a way, I am. There has always been an easy intimacy between us. I do not believe it is because I was born deaf, like him, but rather because we are similar in spirit. Also, I think it endears me to him that I take after his mother, Lila Lambert, in physical appearance. Like her, I am slender with sunlight-colored hair and hazel eyes.

Sam is in the kitchen too, warming by the fire. He is white with red spots and brown eyes. Pushing away my upset, I sign "sit," and Sam does. Papa and I have taught him a dozen signs. Eamon usually keeps him well-brushed, but I gently pull a few burrs from his coat as I pet him.

Normally, Mama doesn't want him in the house. But she is not paying attention. She is staring longingly across the kitchen at George's bedroom.

Papa and I see what she's doing. He takes Mama's hand and gently pecks her on the cheek, before washing and sitting down at the table.

I serve the chicken and vegetable soup and join Mama and Papa.

"Mr. Butler said a young scientist is visiting Chilmark, as Reverend Lee's guest. I saw them walking up from the beach," I sign.

"I have heard the same," Papa signs. "Maybe we should invite him for supper." He looks at Mama, who gives no response.

"John Skiffe is in a rage." Papa tries a new subject. "He's convinced that acres of land the Wampanoag were granted access to in perpetuity by the colonies are his forebear's land, and he's determined to get them back."

If the Wampanoag believe land should be held collectively, they must not understand his claim.

"Over by the Butler farm?" Mama's interest is piqued. "I thought he grazed his livestock there."

"He did for a while," Papa signs. "He squatted on the land rather than owning it."

"Edward," Mama signs, "it's improper to call a neighbor a squatter."

I try not to giggle at Papa's insolence toward Mr. Skiffe.

"Clarissa, I don't like to contradict you," Papa signs sincerely, "but we all started as squatters on this island. In this dispute, the Supreme Court has come down in favor of the Wampanoag of Gay Head."

"They often change their rulings," Mama reminds him.

I look at Mama. Her eyes appear worried; blue sky with dark clouds.

"True," Papa signs thoughtfully.

"Young Wampanoag men intimidate us!" Mama insists. "Knocking down fences the Church guardians build to unlawfully graze their livestock."

"No Wampanoag have harmed us," Papa signs calmly. "I would not let that happen."

Is Mama scared of all Wampanoags? Is she scared of Thomas? Isn't he our friend?

Mama nods at Papa and gives a weak smile.

When we finish eating, Mama and I clear the table, while Papa stokes the fire.

As I wash the dishes, I tell myself a story about a girl who lives alone in a castle on a distant star where everything glows. The only way that she can communicate with others is with a spyglass. She signs and then looks through the glass to watch for a reply. At night, when the sun is away, it is too dark to see the person on the other end of the spyglass. How can she help but feel all alone?

Chapter Eight

I wake up feeling jittery.

There is a cold nip in the air even inside. I dress in my green wool gown and black stockings. I wrap my shawl tight around my shoulders and pull my mobcap over my ears.

I have lost my confidence about following through with Nancy's plan. If Mama found out, she could no more forgive me for the haunting than for luring George into the road. And what would Reverend Lee make of my blasphemy?

While I long for a chance to see George one last time and ask forgiveness, what if he is angry with me? What if his spirit makes demands on me, like Nancy's grandmother Edith did of her?

I go downstairs, yawning like a lion. Mama is gathering ingredients to bake bread. It's one household chore I do well. She hands me an apron to pin to the front of my gown, and we begin mixing the water, yeast, and salt. I am glad for the distraction. And I am grateful that Mama buys our wheat flour from a miller in Tisbury so we don't have to grind it ourselves.

With our bare hands, we knead the dough, over and again, over and again. We put the kneaded dough in a bowl and cover it with a wet cloth. In an hour's time, it will rise.

Mama settles in Grandma Harmony's rocking chair by the fire and takes up a pair of Papa's trousers to mend. As I trace the grain on the kitchen table with my index finger, I try spinning a tale, but my mind is too occupied to create. I busy myself with sweeping instead. And the thought comes to me: George would want me to try to commune with him. If some part of him remains, he might be lost and afraid.

When at last the final proving of the bread is done, we shape it into loaves and place them in cast-iron pans on the hearth.

After a few minutes, I check them. Mama taught me what her mother taught her. "Let it rise until it cracks open." They are not yet done.

I jump when Mama taps me on the shoulder.

"Go," she signs, sensing my impatience. "Remind Nancy to come for supper tonight. Her mother will be visiting a sick cousin. She's to spend the night with us."

"Thank you, Mama," I sign.

My heart races as I pull on my coat and hat and walk the high road toward the turn for Littlewoods Lane. Wind with a drizzle of rain whips my bare face. My nose starts to run. Soon I am wet up to my calves. It's cold as a witch's breath. I wiggle my fingers and toes to keep feeling in them. Cattails scratch at my stockings. Fish and salamanders skirt by me, making me gasp. I jump over a small channel.

When Nancy sees me coming, she waves. I hurry down to meet her.

"Phew," Nancy signs, wiping her brow. "I didn't think you'd come."

"I am ready," I tell her even as I feel waves of nausea and trepidation.

"Here, sheets," she signs, holding them up.

I wonder where Nancy got them, but I don't ask. They are worn and a bit dirty, but they are not in terrible condition. Mama would see nothing wrong with the state of these sheets. She always says, "Waste not, and ye will want not." I don't envy Helen, who does the Skiffes' laundry. Very few things seem to please Mrs. Skiffe. She must have discarded these.

Nancy hangs her cloak and hat on a tree clear of the dark, sinking marsh.

I begin to wrap her like a corpse, but she keeps signing, "I am a soldier who died in the War for Independence. I've come back to avenge my British killers and claim this land as mine once again!"

I knew Nancy would concoct a scheme. Whenever George followed us on our walks, he was amused by her inventions.

"Stay still," I sign.

I put the sheet around her face and drape it over her shoulders. I wind the rest around her limbs. In profile, with her face obscured and one cloaked arm raised, she looks ghastly.

When I am done, Nancy continues to weave her story. She is signing boisterously, "I am not easy in my grave. No one remembers to mourn me." I am close enough to feel her howls.

Nancy stops her story to wrap me. She is less careful than when I wrapped her.

I suddenly feel like I can't breathe.

"Wait!" I sign frantically.

"What?" she asks.

Images of George's last ride to the cemetery flash in my mind. I open my hands, searching for words, but simply curl my fingers closed again.

"Are you okay?" Nancy signs.

I close my eyes, take a deep breath, and nod as I will the images to recede.

Nancy finishes wrapping me. Once we are both concealed, we glide, arms extended. Initially, our footfalls are awkward. What clumsy spirits we are! Then we throw up our hands, skipping and twirling until we reach the outskirts of Littlewoods, where thickets of small trees border the marsh.

There are many ghost stories on the island, most about the war or the sea, and some about little lights in the marsh at night. Ezra Brewer called them will-o'-the-wisps, mischievous spirits who try to lead travelers astray. I am trying to lead a spirit home.

"For George," I remind Nancy as I dance. It comforts me to imagine him near again, if just for a little while.

Once, George told me that he had seen a ghostly figure in the yard. As I peered out the window, he exited the kitchen door and circled around the house. With a lantern lighting his face from below, he popped up in the window, looking like a proper specter. I jumped like a spooked cat, and he laughed so hard tears formed in his eyes. I was cross with him and called him a mule. But after a moment, I laughed as well. I wonder if George is laughing at me now.

I watch Nancy prance about as the sun starts to go down behind the trees. It gets dark so early nowadays. We must make quite a spectacle in the dimming light.

I see Nancy's mouth move. I don't know how loudly she moans. I open my mouth and let out a howl too. I am usually embarrassed to make vocal sounds because I cannot hear myself, and I know from seeing people's reactions that I don't sound pleasant. But no one knows it is me beneath my shroud.

I am a spirit. I am a will-o'-the-wisp. I am calling George! I pray for a sign from him.

I wail. My limbs writhe.

Nancy suddenly grabs my arm and pulls the sheet off my head.

"What's wrong?" I ask.

"A trap passed down the lane," she signs. "I heard the horse whinny and saw the driver come to a halt before riding on. They must have seen us and heard our wild howling."

"Oh no!" I sign. "Did you see who it was?"

Nancy nods. "Reverend Lee!"

"Tell me it wasn't him," I implore.

"I recognized the trap and horse," Nancy signs.

We are mortified. Frantically, we remove our shrouds.

"What do we do with these now?" I ask.

"Bury them in the marsh," she signs.

Since George did not make his spirit visible, this feels like a chance to lay him to rest.

I nod.

We fold the sheets and carry them as close as we dare to the marsh.

Nancy pushes her sheet down in the mud with a long stick. She signs, "Here lies General John Wright, finally laid to rest."

"Amen," I sign, playing along. It helps ease my burden to imagine this is all just a game.

Now it's time for my sheet.

I take the stick and try to push it down. It's harder than it looked watching Nancy. The sheet forms a bubble of swampy water and won't easily sink. I keep pushing and poking it, but it gets caught in the reeds.

Nancy comes to my aid. She drags the sheet back to the main water hole without getting caught in thick mud.

"Why won't he go down easily?" I ask. "Is he that perturbed? Does he hate me? I am sorry, my brother, for my sin. I didn't mean to lure you into the high road. Why did you push me out of the way? It should have been me . . ."

Nancy's face whitens, as if she's looking at a specter. I quickly turn around to see if George is behind me. The air is empty. That's when I realize she didn't know. Even though I once accidentally mentioned his expression before he died, Nancy never could have imagined I was responsible for my brother's death.

I can almost see her mind working. Is she putting the pieces together? She composes herself, like a true best friend.

"Mary," she signs. "It wasn't your fault. Besides, George would have chosen saving you over himself."

I push myself up on the long stick to force the winding shroud under the water for good. "Here lies . . . ," I begin, but cannot finish.

We both bow our heads in a moment of silence.

"Amen," Nancy signs, as if I had completed my thought.

I close my eyes and a few tears stick in my eyelashes. I wipe my hands together to clean off the dirt, then make the sign for "finish." "It's late. We should be getting back."

Nancy nods and takes my hand. We walk in silence, my mind full.

To my surprise, I notice that I do feel a little lighter, as if something has been lifted from me.

Is my brother at rest? Or have I finally unburdened myself of my darkest secret by sharing it with Nancy?

As we approach my house, we see Reverend Lee's cart. We look at each other, horrified.

Chapter Nine

When we enter the house, I grab Nancy's hand. The reverend and the young scientist are talking with Mama and Papa. I catch my breath. Up close, he looks so startlingly like George that I wonder for a moment if we could have actually resurrected him! Is he a revenant?

When the lithe frame moves, the illusion is broken.

I notice six chairs at the table. We haven't had dinner guests since George died.

I take off my cloak, hat, and shoes. Nancy does the same. Our clothes and hair are untidy, but no one seems to notice. Mama and Papa must be preoccupied with our guests because they don't ask where we've been or why we're so late getting back.

Reverend Lee interprets for the young stranger.

"Salutations," he says, extending his hand to Papa, "I am Andrew Noble."

Papa introduces me and Nancy. The newcomer gives us a cordial bow.

"Andrew's father, John, and I were at seminary together," Reverend Lee signs and speaks. Reverend Lee is a kindly man, so tall and thin, he seems to sway in a strong breeze like the branches of a beetlebung tree. Like the tree, the top of his head is rounded, and he stoops a bit.

"John left Andover to return to his home in Greenwich, Connecticut. And, well, here I am."

"Are you going on to study the clay cliffs in Gay Head?" Papa asks Andrew, with Reverend Lee interpreting. "Others have come from the mainland to behold their majesty."

"No," Andrew says, laughing. He turns away from Papa and directs his response toward Mama and Reverend Lee.

That is considered rude in our society. I'll excuse him because he is unaware of our customs. There must be fewer deaf people where he comes from.

"I am more interested in facts than a fetching view." Andrew Noble sits upright with his head tilted backward, giving off an air of self-importance. If Ezra Brewer were here, he would roll his eyes.

Mama leads the group back toward the kitchen.

I see Papa pick marsh grasses out of Nancy's hair. He stares at it and then at Nancy. She blushes and stammers with her hands. Papa looks at her for a moment before turning to the others. I feel my face flush. Does he suspect us?

The kitchen looks livelier than it has in months, with polished silver candlesticks and laundered napkins. As I am helping Mama lay out the dishes, she eyes me and then the table.

I look down, feeling guilty that she had to prepare the meal and polish the silver without my help. When I look up again to make eye contact with her, she already has her head bowed in prayer.

After Reverend Lee's benediction, Mama and I serve lobster, mussels, and corn. I wonder if Andrew will like our island fare. Having missed afternoon tea, I am hungry.

As I eat, I examine Andrew. He is older and spindlier than George. His waist is probably smaller than

Mama's. He has blue eyes; not quite as light as Mama's and George's, nor as dark as Ezra Brewer's. I like his hair. It's dark with waves swept back from his smooth forehead. His hands, with long fingers, show no signs of hard labor.

"What brings you to the Vineyard, then?" Papa asks Andrew.

Mama pushes her chair back from the table so she can interpret spoken words for me and Papa, and sign language for Andrew. Nancy and Reverend Lee listen and watch.

Reverend Lee shifts in his chair and wrings his hands. Why is he anxious? Does he know what Nancy and I have done? Will he tell our parents?

"As it happens," Andrew Noble says, "I met a man who visited your island and had quite a story to tell. I wanted to see for myself, so my father wrote a letter of introduction to his school friend Reverend Lee, and I traveled here by schooner."

Andrew is answering Papa's question but again speaking directly to Mama. Why won't he address Papa?

"There are many stories from the island," Mama signs and speaks. "You shouldn't believe all of them."

Papa, Nancy, and I turn toward Andrew with curiosity.

Andrew continues, "The sailor in the New Haven tavern explained to me that there are a large number of deaf and dumb in your town. I can see for myself that is true."

"It has always been that way," Nancy blurts out, expressing what I'm thinking. "At least, since Mary's great-great-grandfather Jonathan Lambert arrived on the island."

Andrew glances at Nancy in a way that makes me realize he is the kind of person who thinks children should be seen rather than heard. Mama has commented on Nancy's poor manners in the past, but now looks at her more sympathetically.

"It is true," Mama signs. "It is nothing unusual."

"Perhaps not for you," Andrew says, "but I have never seen the likes of it. I intend to discover the cause of the deafness on your island."

A good interpreter does not censor for his audience

and lets them draw their own conclusions. But I wonder if Mama feels awkward interpreting Andrew's speech.

"Surely, the deaf exist elsewhere," Reverend Lee signs. He quotes Romans, "O the depth of the riches both of the wisdom and knowledge of God! How unsearchable are his judgments, and his ways past finding out!"

"They don't exist in great number elsewhere," Andrew perseveres. "And most of them reside in asylums or beg for alms on the street. They are not capable of earning their keep."

Now I think Andrew Noble is the one telling stories.

Why should the deaf be different anywhere else? Why shouldn't they be seamen like Ezra Brewer or run sheep farms like Papa and Mr. Skiffe?

When Eliza Smith's widowed father kept climbing on his barn roof, believing he could soar like a hawk, he was sent to an asylum in Boston. But what does that have to do with the deaf?

I glance at Papa. He does not seem as shocked and confused as I am. He doesn't even seem surprised by our visitor's wild ideas. There is a stillness in him. When I catch his eye, he reaches out and pats my hand.

No one replies. Andrew glances around the table. His nervous smile shows he knows he has made a misstep.

"I meant no offense to you and your family, madam. I am grateful for your hospitality," he says, looking at Mama, and then at Reverend Lee. "You make me feel at home after my long, weary travels. Your fine, simple cooking reminds me of my own dear mother's."

Mama seems to soften at his words. "Thank you," she replies. Is it Andrew's resemblance to George that enchants her? I find Andrew's notions of the mainland compared with our island rather grand. We prefer straightforwardness to dupery in Chilmark. Has Mama forgotten this?

Andrew Noble continues. "It is a marvel that you can keep up cheer and live such a civilized life away from the lively activity of Boston."

"My goodness, did Andrew and I catch a fright driving here!" Reverend Lee says, changing the subject. "We were passing the old marsh when I heard a loud moaning in the woods. At first, I thought it must be a poor bear or deer caught in a trap, but as I slowed my cart, I caught sight of two apparitions floating among the trees. They appeared as luminous specters."

I am frozen in my seat. I dare not look at Nancy for fear one of us will show a sign of our guilt.

Mama glances at Andrew Noble. "Did you see it too?" she asks.

"I am interested in facts," he repeats. "But there was certainly something there. Perhaps it was swamp gas. It is said to cause such phenomena when an interaction with natural galvanic impulse—say, lightning—occurs. I can assure you, it is of a very earthly origin."

I quietly exhale.

I turn to sign only to Nancy, but suddenly, Andrew and Reverend Lee jump up from the table. The dishes rattle and water splashes from my mug.

Mama signs quickly to Papa, "Outside, sounds like skirmish."

Papa runs with Reverend Lee to the front door, the rest of us following.

It is dark and raining, with bright, intermittent flashes of lightning. From the doorway, I can make out two men struggling between our house and the farm. Nancy grabs me from behind and points at a cart and horse standing in the rain. They belong to her father.

Reverend Lee runs toward the men. Is he shouting? No one is interpreting for him. Papa is running too. I glance at Mama, who is holding her arms tightly around her body. She tries to pull me inside, but I run after Papa. Nancy follows. I look behind me and see Andrew standing with Mama in the doorway.

Papa seizes Mr. Skiffe under his arms and tries to hold him still. He was tussling with Thomas. They are both mud-splattered. Eamon tries to wrestle Thomas back to the farm, while Papa drags Mr. Skiffe to our house.

Mr. Skiffe knocks his head backward and hits Papa in the face. Abruptly Papa lets go. Reverend Lee goes to his side.

I see Mr. Skiffe sign violently to Papa, "Your freedman is lying! That Indian wife of his stole bedsheets right from under our noses! She is a conniving, thieving woman, and her husband is no better! After all that we have done for her and her daughter too!"

Bedsheets?

I look to Nancy. She is pale and drawn, backing away and shrinking into the shadows.

Did Nancy steal our haunting sheets? Did *we* steal them?

As Eamon leads Thomas toward the farm, I see the barn door is open, a lantern lit inside. Helen's willowy figure is standing in the light. She steps forward, wrapped in a raccoon fur robe, her hair loose. Is Sally with her? What must they be thinking?

I tug on Papa's sleeve and sign frantically, "It's not true! It's not true! Mrs. Skiffe discarded the sheets! We used them to create winding shrouds for the spirits in the Littlewoods! Oh, Papa, stop him!"

Papa gives me a surprised stare. Mr. Skiffe doesn't see my confession, but I believe that Nancy, Reverend Lee, and Mama do.

Papa struggles to restrain Mr. Skiffe and hauls him toward the house. Mr. Skiffe's boot heels drag in the mud and his arms are pinned, so he can no longer sign his nasty accusations. Reverend Lee follows, imploring him as gently as he can to be quieted and be at peace. From the look on Mr. Skiffe's face, I think he will be no such thing.

Mama and Andrew retreat to the house as well. Waves of nausea pass over me and my hands tremble. The rain is coming down in slick sheets now. Everyone has gone in except for me and Nancy, who is shaking.

I gesture for her to follow me into the house.

"You told them!" she signs at me angrily.

"Had no choice," I sign.

"Had no choice?" She emphasizes each word as she signs. "How about keeping silent to protect me?"

"Would you have an innocent woman take the blame?" I ask.

"She is just an Indian," Nancy signs. "What do you think will happen to me when Mother finds out I took the sheets without permission and committed blasphemy in the woods?"

I think about Nancy's words "just an Indian." "I don't know," my hands stammer. I am soaked to the skin and without words. What have I done?

I walk to the front door and look back at my friend with her angry, clenched fists. Nancy hesitates, but she comes and slips in behind me before I close the door. In the kitchen, Mr. Skiffe is raving with his hands. He is using ugly, ugly words for Thomas and his family, words that I do not want to know or see.

Papa won't meet my eyes. Mama makes a pot of tea. Reverend Lee leaves to fetch Mrs. Skiffe at her cousin's house. Mama talks to Andrew. He takes her hand. Does she interpret my confession for him? What must he think?

Nancy sneaks out of the kitchen. I follow her, glad to be away from Mr. Skiffe. She heads to the front of the house and climbs the stairs.

In my room, we strip down to our shifts and mobcaps. Sitting on my bed, I cover myself with the patchwork bedcovers that Mama made for me. Nancy takes up my shawl and paces back and forth.

I sign, "Why didn't you tell me you stole the sheets? Did you intend for Helen to take the blame?"

"I *borrowed* the sheets," she signs. "I didn't think Mother would notice they were missing."

"You won't be honest with me, even now?" I sign.

"I did it for you!" she signs.

I am taken aback. I put my hands up to sign, but no words come.

"Your parents believe in moral correction," she signs. "My parents believe in caning!"

I shudder.

It is true. My parents' anger and disappointment can scald, but they spare the rod. I have seen ugly bruises on my friend in the past. Mama shares my concern but says she cannot interfere with another family's child rearing.

"I wish I could prevent that," I sign.

"Now it appears my father made a false accusation, in front of your father and Reverend Lee. He hates to be wrong. He hates Indians. If you do not recant your confession, he will blame me."

"Then I'd be lying. And what about Hel—"

Nancy interrupts me again, "Then tell me why I shouldn't tell what you've been hiding from your grieving parents?"

The image of my parents, especially Mama, finding out I was responsible for George's death grips me in a vise. "That would be cruel."

With that, the rage seems to go out of her. She climbs under the patchwork covers and turns her back to me. We used to sleep side by side, holding hands.

As I lay staring at the ceiling, I wonder what's going on downstairs and if the Richards family is safe in the barn and if Nancy will betray my secret.

Chapter Ten

When I awake, there is an emptiness in the featherbed next to me. Nancy is gone. It is Sunday, and I quickly dress for church and go downstairs. Mama is alone, busying herself in the kitchen. She doesn't kiss my cheek or forehead.

What if Nancy told my parents about me and George? What do I say? When Mama turns to me, she signs formally, "Eat now. Your father wants to speak with you."

I wait for her to say more, but Mama sits in Grandmother Harmony's rocking chair and takes up a piece of embroidery. I can hardly swallow my porridge. Will Papa be angry? Will I be punished?

"Church, go you?" I sign, changing the subject.

Mama shakes her head, puts down her embroidery, and signs, "There is too much to be done here."

There are no pressing chores to be done on the Sabbath. Mama has not gone to the Meeting House since George died. Will she visit George's grave? Walking out of the kitchen, my feet feel heavy.

I put on my warmest hat. The brewing storm reflects my raging heart. I stand in a spot of warm sunshine at the edge of our farm and wait for Papa to pick me up in his oxcart.

Hesitantly, I climb up beside him. He pats my knee but gazes forward. We are often comfortable being quiet together. But I can feel that he is not at peace either.

"Papa?" I ask, touching his arm.

He turns to me.

"I'm worried Nancy's father will cane her for stealing the sheets," I sign. "And Thomas will be punished for scuffling with Mr. Skiffe."

"Honestly, Mary," he signs, "I don't know what you think. It's dangerous to go near the marsh. And pretend to be a specter? I don't understand."

I cannot explain without confessing my guilt, so I don't try.

I look down.

He lifts my chin.

"To answer your question," he continues, "John

Skiffe is still convinced Helen took the sheets. I'll defend Thomas at council next week and explain it was self-defense. I will make sure he'll only receive a small fine for fighting with John. He will stay on at the farm. There will be gossip."

I must look hopeless. Papa winks and signs, "There will always be gossip." Then he adds, "We will discuss your punishment tomorrow. Today is the Sabbath. Repent."

Chapter Eleven

The Methodist Episcopal Church does not yet have its own building, so we meet at the white clapboard Meeting House, just a half mile from our farm. The two entrances are framed by pilasters. Reverend Lee stands between them, greeting parishioners.

I sneak past him as I enter. What must he think of me after my confession?

I also avoid Andrew, who, to my relief, does not notice me.

We are all seated in rows on wooden benches. We are all Americans of English origin, not Wampanoag or Irish. They have separate houses of worship.

Every week, before Reverend Lee leads the Sabbath service, we hold our town meeting. It is conducted in sign language and spoken English. Children are not permitted to speak, which feels unfair. But at least everyone is invited to town meetings—to air all matters—unlike town council, which rules on specific matters that involve penalties and fees such as the theft of the Skiffes' sheets. The council never holds its meetings on the Sabbath.

Mr. Pye, today's mediator, bangs a gavel on the lectern, then calls on Mr. Skiffe.

Mr. Skiffe stands to sign. "Everyone here knows I had claim on that acreage, as my father did before me," he signs. "The Church deemed it so. Why should it be given to the Wampanoag now?"

Mr. Skiffe has sobered up, though it looks as if his mood is still foul. Mrs. Skiffe, who looks like a grown, dour version of her daughter, sits quietly watching her husband.

My best friend is uncommonly still. I try to catch her eye, but her gaze is aimed at the floor. Not even her feet are swinging.

"That's not business for this meeting," Mr. Pye signs and speaks. "The Supreme Court in Boston has made a decision."

"I am sympathetic to John's predicament," Mr. Butler signs. "Who knows what will be taken from us next. Our ancestors purchased the land. That is not in dispute."

It is uncommon for women to speak, but when

Miss Hammond raises her hand, Mr. Pye cedes the floor to her.

"Is it not?" Miss Hammond stands. "There is the question of whether or not those land dealings were fair, and if we took more from the Wampanoag than was offered."

"Ridiculous!" Mr. Skiffe sneers. "A woman would take a softer view of the matter. Haven't we all worked hard and even fought to make this island community our own? I will not be responsible for the alleged sins of the fathers."

Nancy nods. Is she proud of her father's bigoted notions?

"We could begin negotiations with the Wampanoag of Gay Head," Miss Hammond suggests.

"Preposterous," Mr. Butler declares. "We don't recognize them as a sovereign nation. You would have us open the door to compromise? That's the way to lose everything we've gained."

"I do believe in compromise," Miss Hammond replies.

Mr. Skiffe and Mr. Butler make dismissive gestures

toward her, but I find her ideas more sensible than theirs.

"Just a moment," Mr. Pye intercedes. "It is our custom for all recognized persons to be heard. Are there any further grievances that can be resolved at this meeting?"

No one stands or raises a hand.

Mr. Pye signs and speaks, "Neighbors we are and shall remain. In times like these, it is best not to bear resentments, but rather to work together through the challenges our community faces." He bangs the gavel to close the meeting.

It's obvious from the foot stomping and sour faces that some people's feelings are still raw, and they are unhappy with the lack of resolution about the land disputes.

I glance back. Andrew Noble is sitting ramrod with his legs crossed. He looks amused by the proceedings. Is he silently mocking us?

Reverend Lee rises and folks begin to quiet down again.

Ezra Brewer stands beside him. He doesn't consider

himself churchgoing folk, but he likes to interpret Reverend Lee's spoken sermons into sign language in front of the congregation.

Reverend Lee recites, "You are to bring into the ark two of all living creatures, male and female, to keep them alive with you. Two of every kind of bird, of every kind of animal . . ."

Today, it is the story of Noah and the Flood.

Ezra Brewer is having good sport imitating the wind and sea that rocked Noah's Ark, just as a storm batters the windows and shakes the rafters of the Meeting House now. He is very lively in his interpretation of the birds and beasts.

I look around me. Other parishioners are not as appreciative of his creative performance. Andrew looks like he swallowed a bad oyster. Why should Ezra Brewer's sign telling sicken him?

When Ezra Brewer stomps his feet like an elephant some of my hearing neighbors wince. He swings both arms like a trunk and raises them high. He must trumpet loudly because people cover their ears.

I smile when I remember the time Miss Hammond

let us put our hands on her throat while she imitated an elephant's cry.

I look to see if Nancy is smiling too, but she only stares ahead soberly.

Then come the frogs, wolves, whales, and crows. Ezra Brewer is quite partial to crows. Reverend Lee pauses until he is finished with his animal signs and calls. He seems unbothered by Ezra Brewer's interpretation. And while half the congregation looks prim and unamused, the other half, including me, seems to find the sermon, in all its parts, quite enjoyable.

Reverend Lee continues, "It was man's inability to repent that brought on the Flood and God's wrath. He saw mankind's greed and discord. This is not just a story of old. It echoes the inability to sympathize with one another that we see around us today. Even the best person can be tempted into bad deeds. Remember that. I say to thee, amen."

Was I tempted into a bad deed? I feel ashamed.

I look to Nancy again, but her parents whisk her away, which is fine because I have no idea what I would say to her.

In her absence, I am trapped by Sarah Hillman and Carrie Tilton. We have not seen each other much since school finished at the end of the summer. I believe Carrie also longs for better education for girls. She is the best mathematics student in our class. With the right training, she could rival the boys at Edgartown Academy.

"I am learning candle making with my dear mother," Sarah signs and speaks. "Have you made candles?"

I shake my head.

"I have," Carrie signs. "We use the tallow from our sheep. Once it is heated, we pour it into molds."

"I have seen Mama do that," I tell Carrie.

"Maybe she will show you," Carrie suggests.

I think that would be tedious for me and Mama, but I don't say so.

"We don't use tallow anymore," Sarah says, with an air of superiority. "We use oil from sperm whales now. It produces the best candles."

That is the newest way to make candles. But not everyone has sperm oil in their house or whalers in their family. Manners prevent me from saying what I think about her sperm oil candles.

"Oh," Carrie signs, looking embarrassed. "I didn't know."

I smile at her before I excuse myself to look for Papa.

I watch Reverend Lee introduce Andrew to Miss Hammond and Mr. Pye. He interprets for Andrew and tells them of his intention to discover the cause of the deafness on our island. I notice Papa is watching him too.

What exactly does he mean, he will find the source of our deafness?

Mr. Pye, who is hearing, signs and speaks to Andrew. "We all use the signs. I can't always remember who is deaf and who isn't. What difference does it make?"

"You are being courteous," Andrew says. "Scientific inquiry requires exact data."

Mr. Pye and Miss Hammond nod and politely excuse themselves.

When Andrew meets Mr. Butler, Reverend Lee continues to interpret, "Andrew wants to arrange interviews with the island's residents. Might you be willing?"

Before he can reply, Ezra Brewer steps right up and signs, "Aye, I'll talk to ye and set the story straight."

Andrew Noble seems pleased. Reverend Lee smiles weakly, and Papa winks at me. It is agreed that Reverend Lee will drive Andrew to Ezra Brewer's house and act as their interpreter. I ask Papa if we can go too.

Papa says I may go along if I am under Reverend Lee's care. He must return home to Mama. I know he worries about her.

I aim to see if Andrew talks more about asylums and witness how Ezra Brewer handles him.

Chapter Twelve

Ezra Brewer warms up an old pot of tea and offers each of us a cup. If it wasn't filled with sugar to cover the bitter taste, I would spit out my first sip. Reverend Lee and Andrew Noble hold their cups without drinking, and then set them down next to their chairs.

Ezra Brewer and I position ourselves so we can see Reverend Lee's interpretation.

"My good sir," Andrew says to Ezra Brewer, "I am studying the source of the widespread deafness in your town. As you probably know, any good scientist begins by creating a genealogy of the people he is studying. I hope you can help me with this."

Ezra Brewer nods and launches into a recitation of the Lambert family tree, starting with the arrival of Jonathan Lambert in 1692. He also talks about the Skiffe family, who has more deaf descendants than we do.

I can see that Ezra Brewer is trying not to sign too quickly and to keep his sentences closer to English so

Reverend Lee will not struggle to speak his words to Andrew. Even so, it seems hard for Reverend Lee to keep up with Ezra Brewer's quick spelling on his fingertips.

Eventually, Andrew hands Ezra Brewer a piece of rag paper from his pocket. When he does so, a couple of letters fall to the floor. I am envious of all that paper. If it were mine, I could write down my stories.

Ezra Brewer takes an ink-dipped quill pen and draws a line across the page. Then he draws points along the line and writes down names. He underlines the ancestors he knows for sure were deaf.

He stops to sign, "Not sure some dates."

Reverend Lee interprets, and Andrew assures him it is fine. He is happy to have his help.

I am deeply disappointed that there is no trickery in Ezra Brewer today. He is simply helping Andrew with his research.

After filling a few pages, Ezra Brewer hands back the papers.

"My dear sir," Andrew says, "do you have a notion as to how your infirmity came to be so widespread in these parts?"

Do I see Ezra Brewer wince at the use of the sign for "infirmity"? We use a similar sign for "sickness" and "disease." Deafness is not an affliction. The only thing it stops me from doing is hearing.

Ezra Brewer rubs his hands together to warm them up. A sure sign he is getting ready to tell a colorful story. My heart lifts.

"Let me think when it all began," he signs, with Reverend Lee interpreting.

"Yes, I think it started in England, where the deaf settlers came from. Although there is some talk that they caught the 'infirmity' coming across on the great voyage."

I have never heard that theory. Reverend Lee looks surprised as well, but he is too polite to interrupt Ezra Brewer.

Andrew asks Ezra Brewer, "Did they seem to have the effects of scurvy or other known illnesses?"

Ezra Brewer signs, "I've suffered from scurvy myself. Had to suck on lemons for weeks, I did. Nasty business." He pulls down his lower lip to show us his gums.

Andrew looks impatient.

Ezra Brewer starts signing again, with a twinkle in his eye.

"Now the Black Death is a whole other matter. I have heard of men rendered deaf, dumb, blind, and without taste or smell. They went stark raving mad." Ezra Brewer acts out the effects of the plague like he is a play actor.

"Yes," Andrew says. His red slash of a mouth looks like he has been sucking lemons too. "That is old news. I am here to discover the cause of your deafness."

"Aye, well, there is another theory," Ezra Brewer signs, jerking his head and wiggling his left fingers. "I'd better tell him the story about Widow Merrill." He is addressing me and Reverend Lee.

Reverend Lee begins to ask what story, but I nod my head and sign, "Yes, tell him the story."

I don't know what Ezra Brewer will sign next, but I can't wait to see!

Ezra Brewer works his jaw and leans forward, so the fire gives his grizzled face a glow.

"It was the old Widow Merrill who related the

terrible story. While she was pregnant with her second child, she went to the funeral of a neighbor. At the grave, a strange-looking young lady caught her attention. She looked otherworldly, especially her eerie gray eyes.

"Someone told Widow Merrill that the young lady was deaf. Widow Merrill had never met anybody with this 'infirmity' before. She was from Boston, not our island.

"Widow Merrill watched the young lady closely. When the coffin was lowered, she threw up her hands, raised her eyes, and uttered such a cry that turned Widow Merrill bone white."

Ezra Brewer clasps his hands, and I feel him shriek at the top of his lungs. Reverend Lee and Andrew Noble almost fall off their chairs.

Ezra Brewer signs, "The image of the young lady and the sound of the cry were never far from Widow Merrill after that day. In due time, her second child was born. As she feared, the boy was deaf as a stone. And when he was surprised or scared, he'd give an unnatural cry!"

I brace myself in case Ezra Brewer shrieks again, but he does not.

Ezra Brewer leans back so his face is obscured in the growing darkness and rests his hands in his lap. I imagine he is smiling, pleased with himself.

Andrew Noble seems spooked but angry too.

"I am a man of science, not small-town superstitions," he tells Reverend Lee, who is still interpreting his speech. Andrew is no longer looking at me or Ezra Brewer.

Andrew says, "I'm sure there is a much more reasonable explanation for the infirmity in your town, and I intend to discover it."

"Others have tried before you," Ezra Brewer signs, with a wink and a nod at Reverend Lee. "Pride cometh before a fall."

"I am wasting my time with this nonsense," Andrew replies.

Andrew's manner unsettles me. I see him lean forward in his chair with his fists clenched so tightly in his lap that I'm certain his fingernails must be leaving marks in the soft part of his palm. Although Reverend Lee is always sympathetic, I can tell he's embarrassed when Andrew storms back to the trap, without thanking Ezra Brewer.

The ride home is uncomfortable. Andrew carries on to Reverend Lee while I sit silent. I don't know if his arm waving or cross-armed sulking is more petulant. I have seen colicky infants who are less irritable. Even though I was raised on a farm, I was taught to admire and respect learned people. I admit I am having trouble with this one.

Chapter Thirteen

The next day, after breakfast, Mama informs me that she and I are taking a walk to the Meeting House. I wash and dress slowly as a snail, as I fear what Mama's stiff manner might mean. Is my reckoning nigh for haunting in the woods? But why the Meeting House?

By the time we arrive, I am frozen to the bone and filled with dread. The feeling increases when we enter the Meeting House and I see Nancy. Our broken friendship saddens me. She showed compassion when I shared my darkest secret. Why couldn't she have told the truth about the sheets?

To make matters worse, Nancy appears to have lost none of her spite. Her eyes narrow on me, even as she politely greets Mama. She and Mrs. Skiffe are already seated with Reverend Lee.

He announces, "I'd like to speak to the girls alone."

Our mothers go to the antechamber. I don't see what Mrs. Skiffe signs to Nancy, but I imagine it's similar to Mama's signed instructions to "behave honorably" and "straighten your bonnet."

Reverend Lee gestures for us to sit in front of him. He opens the Bible to a page he's marked with a worn ribbon. Then he closes it and rests it on his robed knee. He removes his spectacles and searches our waiting faces.

"Do you understand that blasphemy means not only speaking against Our Lord but also committing acts of impiety or godlessness?" he asks us.

We both nod earnestly.

"I believe you do. So I cannot reckon how you thought that mocking the dead in their winding shrouds would not put your souls in mortal peril. Can you tell me?"

I look to Nancy. I truly don't know what to say. I can't tell the truth about George.

Seeing that I am silent, Nancy's brown eyes spark and focus.

"How could we mock our poor, lost dead ones?" she signs. She looks directly into his kind blue eyes. "On the night my grandmother Edith died, I received a visitation at the foot of my bed. Her lustrous glow lit the room. Before passing on, she wanted to convey a message of love to me. I was moved that she thought of reassuring me before her soul ascended."

Reverend Lee is fascinated by the tale.

She continues. "Mary has been deeply troubled by her only brother's untimely death. We thought we might find some remnant of his spirit and commune with him for comfort and peace if we dressed as he last appeared in this world. We thought Our Lord would understand our true meaning as He sees into our hearts at all times."

Reverend Lee pauses for a moment. His brow is knitted as he opens and closes his Bible and rubs the ribbon.

Finally, he signs, "Well, well. I can see you have thought a great deal about your sin. I am relieved to know that you realize God observes you and divines your true intentions *at all times*." He is not a fool, but he may also remember childish games, and he knows the hardship my family has faced.

"I believe you do fully comprehend your sins," he signs. "If you agree never again to call to the dead on land the Church has not consecrated, we can let the matter rest."

We nod somberly and cross our hearts.

As Reverend Lee traverses the room to talk with our mothers, I turn to Nancy so no one else sees my words. "You didn't tell my secret."

"That would have been cruel," she signs. "Though I don't like you taking the Indians' side against me."

I look at Nancy. She's sullen but not bitter.

"Are we still friends?" I ask.

"I have no other choice," she signs. "I certainly don't want to fall in line behind Sarah Hillman the way Carrie does." Do I detect a twinkle in her eye?

"I need your help," I tell her. "I want to know what Andrew Noble is up to."

Nancy nods and rubs her chin. "Spying?" she asks hopefully.

I sign, "There may be no other way."

Chapter Fourteen

A few days later, Papa tells me that Andrew Noble has taken a census of the different towns on the island. After officially counting people on Martha's Vineyard, Andrew has decided to focus on Chilmark. We have the highest number of deaf residents. I hadn't noticed that before. He concluded that one in four residents of Chilmark is deaf compared with one in six thousand on the mainland. You might have knocked me down with a feather! Are we that far apart? There is only a small strip of Atlantic Ocean between us.

Papa also told me that Andrew has been collecting soil from our land and water samples from our wells. What does he plan to do with his findings? What will happen to our island if he does find the source of our deafness? I imagine our shores overrun by observers, stomping through our farmlands and asking impertinent questions. Caravans of explorers will arrive to visit the land of the deaf! We have no leopard skins or ivory tusks. What trophies will they take away with them?

But isn't that what the first white settlers did to the Wampanoag? Reverend Lee reminded us in a sermon that earliest contact resulted in Wampanoag men being captured and sold as slaves in Spain. I feel less impressed by our forefathers, even as I cherish our island.

I meet Nancy on the high road near the parsonage at our agreed time. She looks at me and frowns, raising her eyebrows and snapping the fingers of both hands, the way a hearing person might cluck their tongue. "Your frock," she signs.

"What's wrong with it?" I counter, smoothing my hands over my skirt.

"It's too bright," she chastises. "Don't you know anything about spying? You have to merge with the landscape."

I grab the edges of my cloak and pull them tightly around me. I have no choice but to wear all my winter garb on this frosty day. "I'll just keep myself hidden," I tell her. She looks unconvinced.

On our hands and knees, we duck behind the stone wall and wait. Mama will sigh when she sees the dirt on my clothing. Though I've been this way all my life, she has never grown used to it.

As we hoped, Andrew Noble exits the parsonage and, paying us no mind, strides confidently down the high road, carrying his black satchel. Nancy raises her eyebrows at me again and signs, "Bag?"

"His equipment," I reply. I am sad for a moment, thinking of George; he collected things in his pockets and brought them home to examine on the kitchen table. In Andrew Noble, I see what he could have been: professional, scientific. But never as ill-mannered.

"He is interested in facts!" Nancy exclaims, and we both snicker.

We crawl along for a little way, Nancy peeking her curly head up over the wall every now and again to track him. I tell myself I will not make light of Nancy's spying efforts in the future.

Andrew Noble stops on the other side of the road, placing his satchel on the stone wall. He takes out a small shovel and a phial. He digs up dirt and puts it into a glass jar.

We watch him do this at different locations, each time placing the glass jar in his bag. But when he uses a paring knife to take a sample of the bark of an apple tree, Nancy is so indignant at the defilement, I have to grab her and hold her back.

In the distance, I see Andrew's schooner against the bright autumn sky and gray sea. Has he really been in Chilmark less than a week?

Nancy stops suddenly and points. Ezra Brewer is standing in the road smoking his pipe. Nancy turns to me. "Perfect," she signs. "Let's go stand with Ezra Brewer. Sometimes the best spying can be done right in plain sight. Keep your eyes open."

Ezra Brewer is watching with open curiosity as Andrew takes samples of the sand and soil. He removes his pipe, shakes his head, and puffs out his lips, like a horse snorting.

When we join him, I rub my fingers together, making our sign for "dirt." "Do we eat it?" I ask Nancy. "You walk on it the same as me and Papa and Ezra Brewer, and yet you hear."

Ezra Brewer rolls his eyes. "That man might as well investigate whether the Archangel Gabriel blows a deafening trumpet into the ears of selected infants on the Vineyard."

I giggle. Ezra Brewer blows an imaginary trumpet into the air, and Nancy jumps, scowling slightly. She is frightened of him, whether she would admit it or not. I fear Andrew heard the discordant sound. Hopefully, he'll think we are playing a game, rather than watching him.

As the three of us continue to follow him, we sometimes mimic his movements. He stoops to dig clay out of the ground and put it in a bucket. The ground is still wet from Sunday's rain and makes his breeches muddy.

His strides are long. When he slows, we talk together, pretending he is not our main concern. I think Ezra Brewer enjoys the game. I fear that Andrew will turn around and confront us. How could I explain, without seeming like a fool? I'm sure he'd tell Mama I was acting rude and childish.

Rounding a bend, there are a handful of people who make us less conspicuous.

Andrew approaches the reverend's sister-in-law, Mrs. Lee, who is signing in the road with Mrs. Butler.

Mrs. Lee seems to recognize him a moment too late to escape. She tries to avoid him, but he is already saying something to her, removing his hat in greeting.

Mrs. Lee is hearing. I am inclined to believe that at that moment she wished she wasn't. Mrs. Butler has turned away with a sour look on her face.

Nancy edges forward and molds herself to a tree so she can interpret for us. Ezra Brewer and I pretend to sign a conversation while eyeing Nancy's interpretation.

Mrs. Lee's youngest son, Ben, is stomping in a puddle.

Nancy signs, "He is asking her if the child is hearing . . ."

Suddenly, Mrs. Lee looks as if she might smack Andrew Noble! What has he said? I look to Nancy, whose cheeks are coloring deeply. "He asked her if her stays were of a severe tightness while she was with child," Nancy explains, and Ezra Brewer howls with laughter till he chokes on the smoke from his pipe.

When Mrs. Lee and Andrew Noble turn to look at Ezra Brewer, Nancy signals me to run with her behind a bush.

"Why are we hiding?" I sign. "He already saw us."

"Exactly. He won't expect us to follow him. It's the perfect cover. This way we can see what he does next. He probably thinks we just went on our way," she replies.

We peek out from behind the bush. She's right. Andrew is continuing up the high road. What is he up to now?

Chapter Fifteen

We squat behind an oxcart until it turns down a lane. We walk quietly and keep a safe distance. When Andrew stops and turns around, we jump on the stone wall and climb the nearest apple tree. It has dropped its leaves, but the branches are thick and tall. Hopefully, we are merging, like good spies.

I go first and startle when I spot someone sitting on a branch above me. It is Sally Richards!

Her hair is tucked under a mobcap. She wears a brown patterned dress that is too large for her. I recognize it as one of Nancy's old ones. Mrs. Skiffe will only have a Wampanoag girl working under her roof if she looks like a proper English girl.

For a moment, I panic. If Sally is neglecting her duties at the Skiffe household, Nancy will become belligerent. Nancy is now by my side, and she sees Sally. When their eyes meet, they seem neither friends nor enemies.

On the high road, Andrew turns around and comes toward us, stopping under a nearby tree.

We all remain still.

If he looks up, we have been stealthy for naught.

Nancy faces Sally and puts her finger on her lips. Sally nods.

"I've been watching the two of you," Sally signs.

"We've been following him," I admit.

Nancy scowls at my disclosure.

"Why?" Sally asks.

"I distrust him," I sign, opening my fist like I am throwing a stone.

Sally nods and signs, "A person comes, rowing a mishoon or canoe, uninvited. He scouts the land and takes things that don't belong to him."

"Meaning what?" Nancy signs, with a twisted look on her face. I suppose she feels her father is being attacked for his claim on Wampanoag land.

Sally points at Andrew. Nancy huffs.

I'm glad I am sitting in the middle. To ease tension, I sign, "What is he doing?"

We can see only the top of Andrew's head. He seems to be taking another sample from the ground.

"Dung beetles?" Sally guesses.

"Or dung," Nancy signs. It is a sign not used in polite conversation.

The three of us struggle not to burst out laughing.

Just when we cannot hold our breath a moment longer, Andrew picks up his satchel and walks back up the high road with a steady stride.

We climb down. Nancy is still sulky.

"I must return home," she announces.

"Me too," I sign. "Thanks for your help. I'll keep you apprised of further developments."

She softens a bit and walks up the high road.

"Are you going to see your papa at our farm?" I ask Sally.

She nods. I suggest we walk together. Sally hesitates, then agrees.

Even a year ago, I would not be seen walking with her. But if Papa doesn't treat Thomas differently from other men, why should I treat Sally differently from other girls?

I ask her, "What were you doing up in the tree?"

"I need a private place sometimes," she explains.

I take up a birch stick as we walk. After we pass the

Hillman house, I stoop to look at a fallen bird's nest, turning it over with the stick. There are still bits of shell in the dried twigs from when the nestlings hatched. They have probably already flown away for the winter.

Sally crouches to see what I'm seeing. "Spotted sandpiper." She identifies the species by finger-spelling. She also pays careful attention to small, discarded things. That makes her a different kind of companion than Nancy.

Mr. Butler is standing on the stone wall with his spyglass as we pass. He doesn't address me, and I ignore his disapproving glare. I hope Sally doesn't see it.

"Have you entered Bayard's paddock again?" I ask her.

"I have," she signs, smiling. "And he took the new salt lick I gave him."

"But aren't you afraid of him?" I sign.

We stop to watch a black-crowned heron swoop down to snatch a herring from an icy brook.

"No," Sally signs hesitantly. "He's a good horse. He's just wounded. He's lost his young master."

"George," I sign, and lower my hands.

"I have a plan to put Bayard at ease again," Sally signs. "I'm trying to talk Papa into bringing two horses from Aquinnah. We will run Bayard between the good horses until he learns from them."

"Oh, I'd like to see that!" I tell her.

"Maybe one day," she signs dreamily.

When we approach the pastures, I wave to the sheep. They reciprocate by chewing their wheat straw and staring blankly at me. I spell "baa" on my fingers. Sally smiles at my jest.

A shyness comes over us. I am embarrassed that I cannot invite Sally to tea with me and Mama. Will there ever be a time when we can be true friends?

Sally waves while she walks toward the barn. I wave too and head for home.

The kitchen is warm and bright from a blazing fire. Papa is relaxing by the hearth with his pipe, reading the *Farmer's Almanac*. I am startled to see Andrew Noble sitting at the table, talking rapidly at Mama. Why has he returned?

Mama looks up when she sees me. Her eyes shine bright. She looks different. More hopeful, perhaps?

"You're home sooner than I thought," Mama signs and speaks at the same time. She is speaking for Andrew's benefit. This makes her signs more like spoken English and less like our special language.

Before I can respond, Mama turns to Andrew and speaks without signing. I groan inwardly. What is she saying?

After I hang up my cloak, I go over to Papa. I sit on the arm of his chair and lean on him. I read the *Almanac* over his shoulder. We are silent together.

Mama and Andrew go into George's bedroom. He comes out, arms filled with books.

"Those belong to my brother," I sign.

Mama doesn't interpret for Andrew.

She signs, "To aid him in his research. He will return them."

I look to Papa, who frowns but does nothing. I am fuming inside. Why is Mama helping Andrew? Why is she giving this stranger a piece of George? As

Andrew departs, it occurs to me that he probably took the local geography book with the map of memories inside it.

If so, I will have to retrieve it.

Chapter Sixteen

The temperature is dropping. Winter is approaching. In a week, it will be the last month of this painful year.

Andrew brought Mama an amber-tinted piece of sea glass to thank her for the books. She added it to her collection on the kitchen windowsill. He explained that it can take from seven to ten years of wave tumbling to make it. She was impressed. I told her this when I learned it from Miss Hammond. Does Mama not remember? Why is he trying so hard to endear himself to her?

After the monotony of sweeping, Mama asks me to polish the pewter. This is usually only done on special occasions. My plan to retrieve the map makes me too nervous to inquire. Mama is spirited as she does her chores. In the short time since Andrew's arrival, I see a change in her.

Around noon, I am released from my chores. Though no one is there to see me, I tiptoe along the road and keep close to the bushes, occasionally ducking into their scratchy branches. I am being extra cautious without Nancy to guide me.

The parsonage is one of the oldest buildings on the island. Its gray clapboard has been whitewashed and built upon over the years. It sits about halfway between our farm and the Meeting House on a parcel of land that borders the Lees' modest family farm. I have been here before. Mama used to take tea with Reverend Lee and sometimes brought me along.

Reverend Lee must be out visiting because his trap is not here. I see Andrew walking down-island with purposeful strides. I try to merge with the side of the parsonage and discreetly look out.

Carrie's grandmother, the Widow Tilton, helps Reverend Lee keep house. I try to quiet my breathing and hope my stomach doesn't growl because she is hearing. Deaf people can easily make sounds without ever realizing it. George sometimes made teasing remarks about it.

Cautiously, I peek through the kitchen window. Mrs. Tilton is stoking the fire.

I'm certain Nancy would tell me to climb through the window. Instead, I head to the front door at the other end of the house. My heart quickens and my hands sweat as I slowly open it a crack and peek in. Seeing no one, I slip through, carefully latching the door behind me. I stretch my legs from rug to rug as I move down the hall, avoiding footfalls on the wooden floor.

I thought I would remember where things are, but my panic is disorienting me. I clasp my hands to keep them still and look toward the kitchen for Widow Tilton.

She is now in the yard fetching water. At the back of the house, a door to the right of the kitchen is ajar. Maybe it's the guest room? I rush toward it and sneak inside before gently closing the door. I rest against it, my chest rising and falling as I try to still my frantic breathing. Spying is much more taxing than I realized.

The light from the window is thin and gray as it filters through the glass. Freshly cleaned socks hang from the sill. They have been darned many times, and there is the faint smell of old wool in the air. A pair of simple britches is folded over the back of a chair at the desk, and I feel scandalous even looking at them.

On the desk is a curious white object, stiff in stature, sitting in a ring. A clergy collar! I am mortified to realize that I am standing in Reverend Lee's bedroom.

There are few other personal objects. The bed is too small for his long frame. No wonder he stoops. I will have to forget all this when I next see him standing at the pulpit.

I put my hands on the door to feel vibrations. Nothing but quiet. I exit and peek out a window. Widow Tilton is talking with Mrs. Lee.

Stealthily, I cross to a room on the other side of the house.

The bedstead is larger than Reverend Lee's, with a golden cross nailed to the wall above the headboard. A simple washstand with a mirror sits in the corner. The scent from a fancy bottle of hair tonic tickles my nose.

I recognize some of George's books on the floor by the side of the bed. The geography book with the map of memories tucked inside is not among them. But under the window is a desk crowded with more books, jars of samples, and assorted papers. I sift through the meticulous stacks.

I see Ezra Brewer's genealogy, drawings, and columns of numbers that I cannot decipher, but no geography book. Does Andrew have it on his person? Did he discover my map? Why did Mama have to give him that book?

I almost rip off the bedsheets to look for it. Tears fill my eyes, and I breathe heavily. I pray for strength before I go on. Maybe the map is no longer in the book. I turn back to the stacks of papers to look for it and unearth an envelope with a return address in Boston. I slip a letter out of the envelope.

I feel vibrations through the wood floor. What will I say if I am suddenly caught? I have sinned too often lately to keep making up lies.

I swing around. There is no one there.

The vibrations must be my own heart beating in my chest.

"Cowardly spy!" I sign to myself.

Widow Tilton and Mrs. Lee will not stay out in the cold for long, so I must hurry.

I take up the letter and read:

Dear Andrew,

I wish you all the best in your studies.

If your father's old friend is willing to put you up on the island, I recommend that you find lodgings where you can work without interruption.

It's always best to be in the field when researching a subject or people. Try to ingratiate yourself with the natives. It will make the study of their inherent deafness and idiocy more pleasant.

If you are correct, and it is a local element causing the condition, take care not to expose yourself to the source.

When you return to the city, bring back samples and acquire a live specimen, if possible—

Again I feel the floor vibrate. I peer out the door and see Widow Tilton's shadow in the kitchen. She is at the basin washing dishes.

I scold myself for not making a clear picture in my head before I moved things and do my best to replace everything where I found it. I slip out of the bedroom while the Widow Tilton's back is to me.

I hold my breath and press myself up against the wall. It confounds me that hearing people can detect the slightest sound. Widow Tilton turns and looks toward the door. Not seeing anything, she shakes her head and returns to her washing. I take my chance and dash out.

I am careful not to slam the door behind me.

Walking home, I think about the letter. Who wrote it? There are other ignorant people who think as Andrew does?

Sarah Hillman runs out to greet me when I pass her house. Carrie Tilton trails behind her. It gives me a start seeing her after I have just evaded her grandmother.

"You are so lucky to have that young man calling at your home," Sarah signs. I detect a glimmer in her apple-green eyes.

"Why do you say that?" I ask.

"Don't be a silly girl," Sarah signs, acting older than her twelve years. "He's very handsome, with those piercing blue eyes. He isn't a simple island farmer or whaler. He's from the city, and he attended Yale University, even if he didn't finish his studies."

"I don't see it like that," I tell her.

"Oh, you can't fool me," Sarah signs, resting her hand under her tilted chin.

Carrie casts me a sympathetic glance.

"Andrew is ten years older than I," I sign.

Sarah gives me a knowing look, twisting her red curls around her fingers.

"That won't matter when you are eighteen and he is twenty-eight," she signs. "And with your brother gone, your father needs a son to inherit his property. My mother says it's obvious why your family had him over for dinner and has taken an interest in him."

"Not because of me!" I sign.

"Don't play coy with me, Mary Lambert," she signs aggressively. "Everyone is talking about it."

"You stop gossiping about my family!" I sign.

I walk away without a single courtesy. I don't have time for such silliness.

On my way home, I think more about the letter. What is a live specimen?

Chapter Seventeen

Behind the barn, Thomas is sweeping out the sheep shelters and putting in fresh wheat straw. The flock can abide snow but need blocking from the winter winds.

I am still brooding over the missing map and not ready to go inside. I walk over to him. "I saw Sally last week," I tell him.

"She said so," he signs.

"She told me a story," I sign, "about a man who came to the island uninvited, conducted a survey, and took things that didn't belong to him."

He stops working and focuses his attention on me.

"Stories can be interpreted in many different ways," he signs.

"I have heard some arguments about land disputes," I sign. "That our fathers took land that didn't belong to us."

He stops and rubs his chin thoughtfully.

"As far as I am concerned," he tells me, "there have never been any real disputes."

"What do you mean?"

"Missionaries and English settlers have made land claims up and down Noepe," Thomas signs confidently. "It remains a Wampanoag island. In truth, no one can truly buy or sell this land. It belongs to a far greater Being."

"You mean your god, Moshup?" I ask.

"I shouldn't call him a god but rather our greatest ancestor," Thomas signs. "He, not the Church or the Commonwealth, is the only one who gave us a deed to the island. He taught us to be partners with it in respectful stewardship."

"I follow Christian beliefs," I tell him.

"All beliefs are important to the believers," he signs.

"Do you think my family should leave?" I ask Thomas.

"That will not happen," he signs. "We are willing to share. But that doesn't mean you can lay claim to land that was granted to us, or that an honest woman can be falsely accused."

"I told the truth about the sheets," I sign. "I am truly sorry for the part I played in Helen's persecution."

"It was good of you to speak the truth," he tells me. "Just as it was honorable for your father to testify that when I scuffled with an Englishman, it was in self-defense."

"Why does it matter that we are English or Irish or Wampanoag?" I ask him. "We are all Americans now."

"I think you know it's not as simple as that," Thomas signs.

Do I? It's hard to reckon it out in my mind. Sam paws at my leg.

Thomas points toward my house. Mr. Pye's carriage is outside.

I leave Thomas to his work. Sam follows me to the house. Before going inside, I command him to "sit" and give him a good scratch on the rump. His undercoat has grown for the winter, so he is big and bushy. I know he wants to sleep by the fire, but he must sleep in the barn to help keep predators at bay.

When I enter the kitchen, I see that Andrew and Miss Hammond are here too. The hearth is not just well-cleaned and the table well-laid with silver, but festive red candles are aglow, and fresh pine boughs crackle in the fire. Mama instructs me to pour ale for Papa, Andrew, and Mr. Pye in pewter mugs from the cupboard. Will wonders never cease?

There is much fussing over the beautiful preparations as we take our seats. Mama has a right to look proud.

Although it is not my place to ask questions at supper with grown folks, I see this as my chance.

"Mama," I sign, "would you interpret for me? I have a question to ask Andrew."

She looks to Papa, who nods. Andrew is looking at us. No one is interpreting. Mama nods as well.

"I've been watching you conduct your experiments," I tell him.

He guzzles his ale, then wryly replies, with a piercing look, "I have noticed."

Nancy and I were not quite as covert as we had hoped.

"Do you think a local element is causing our deafness?" I ask him.

Andrew looks surprised.

Miss Hammond beams with delight. I am one of her best students. Though my talent lies more in words than scientific problems.

"That is my theory," he responds, looking mostly at Mama. He also glances at me with interest. This is the first time we are conversing, albeit with Mama's help. "I think the well water may have a rare impurity that causes your infirmity."

I cannot tell if Andrew's speech is cordial. Would Mama interpret insults the way Reverend Lee did? Perhaps Andrew is careful not to let her see that side of him.

"We all drink the same water." Mr. Pye signs as fluently as he speaks. He is echoing what I said to Nancy.

"That is true," Andrew says. "There may be an explanation for that."

"Have you seen any similar cases?" Mr. Pye asks.

"My hypothesis," Andrew says rather loftily, "is based on Cadwallader Colden's work on the epidemic of yellow fever. In 1743, he published essays explaining how filthy living conditions were related to high incidence of the disease in New York City."

Mr. Pye says, "I don't see how that's relevant to deafness in Chilmark. It's not a disease, like yellow fever."

"That's a matter of opinion," Andrew says.

Miss Hammond signs and speaks, "Honestly, in all my years I have not heard of any person in this town suffering and dying from the inability to hear."

"I agree," Mr. Pye quickly adds. "In some ways, I have always considered my deaf neighbors luckier for the less than melodious sounds they escape. Roosters, screaming infants, and the like."

Papa laughs broadly. I stifle a giggle. It is common deaf humor on the island to name all the ways that the hearing are disadvantaged.

"Very amusing, sir," Andrew says, ignoring Papa and me, "but wouldn't it be better if these people didn't have to live their lives in a reduced state?"

Papa, Mr. Pye, Miss Hammond, and I stare at Andrew. Mama seems embarrassed to have interpreted it for us but says nothing.

I look at Papa. He is watching intently. Why does he keep quiet? Are his thoughts not appropriate for a polite supper?

I have wondered if Papa feels powerless having his wife speak for him on important matters. There is usually a lovely balance between them. George and I could never turn them against each other in our disputes. But this intruder has tipped the scale in a way I would have never imagined.

I sometimes feel in chats with hearing peers that it can be difficult to put in my own thoughts. They interpret whenever possible, but when they converse in a group, they look and talk only to one another. It is not mean-spirited but careless. They forget to slow down and include me. Is this what Papa is feeling?

"Young man, I am aghast that you would make such an insulting remark under our hosts' roof," Mr. Pye signs and speaks.

I want to stand up and applaud.

"I meant no offense," Andrew says, Mama still signing for him. "We are in the Enlightenment. The purpose of science is not only to better understand the world around us but also to improve the lot of the suffering."

Ever a peacemaker, Papa raises his mug in a toast: "Health good long." Everyone follows his example, but the gathering feels strained.

"What is the desired outcome of your experiments?" Mr. Pye asks sharply.

"Pardon me, sir," Andrew replies, "but I don't understand the question."

Mr. Pye signs and speaks, "If we clean our water supply and other foul living conditions, assuming there are any in Chilmark, do you mean for the deaf to disappear? Is it your opinion that deafness is a scourge to eliminate, like yellow fever?"

"I think the healthier and more whole we are, the better," Andrew says. "We must strive for perfection, not just in nature but among men. Anything less is a poor substitute."

Mama hesitates while interpreting Andrew's last remark. "Please eat," she replies as she quickly changes from interpreter to hostess and takes up her fork to eat after smiling at her guests.

There is a long silence. Mama looks to Papa.

He signs, "My wife prepared a delicious repast. My daughter is impressionable. I don't care for these discussions at my family's table. I don't know what will come of your study of our island, but the Lamberts will no longer take part in it."

Mr. Pye and Miss Hammond are beaming. I can't read Mama's expression.

"At least you all live like Christians," Andrew says, trying to ingratiate himself again.

"Why wouldn't we?" Miss Hammond signs and speaks.

"Why, madam, because you are surrounded by the savage races," Andrew responds.

"They are mostly Christianized," Mr. Pye tells him.

"Yes," Andrew acknowledges, "the Church has done what it can."

"I think the Church has done quite enough," Miss Hammond signs and speaks.

"What I'd like to know," Mama signs and speaks, "is what is to be done with the children of Wampanoag women and freedmen. The Wampanoag complain that we stole their land, even though we paid them for it honestly. Now that the women are giving birth to mongrels, will they still lay claim to Wampanoag land? I don't see how they can."

How can Mama be so cruel? "Mongrel" is a good

way to describe pups, not children. Sally is a girl just like me. Is it Andrew who brings out the worst in Mama?

I think about what Thomas explained to me, that the Wampanoag do not place the same importance on bloodlines as we do, and that the land belongs to Moshup, who shares it with his people.

I look to Papa to add more reason to the discussion. He appears calm, but I sense his strength rising under the surface. Still, I know he will not contradict Mama in front of guests.

Andrew says, "That is a problem, madam. The Commonwealth of Massachusetts has often acted as too permissive a father to his Wampanoag children. I hope they will make sure no group abuses their special privileges."

Mama offers second helpings, and we finish the meal in silence. When everyone is done eating, Mr. Pye and Miss Hammond stand up to leave, making excuses about having to check in on a sick relative.

My dear schoolteacher gives me a hug and signs, "I pray for the well-being of your family."

Andrew also excuses himself. While putting on his coat, he thanks Mama for her hospitality, then kisses her hand and begins his walk back to the parsonage.

For the first time, I wonder, Does being deaf determine my worth? Will deafness ever disappear from the world? Are there really perfect men?

Chapter Eighteen

After I help clean up and say good night, I start to climb the stairs, then stop. I slowly creep back, trying to make my footfalls as quiet as possible. I can feel stomping. I know Mama and Papa are not happy with each other. They never wanted George or me to witness their conflicts. Are they angry with me since I'm the one who started it by prompting Andrew's foul behavior at dinner?

Mama and Papa face each other in the kitchen.

I stand to one side of the doorway. Mama signs at him furiously.

The kitchen is dark save for the fireplace and the candles left on the table from supper. Their signing hands cast long shadows on the wall. I catch parts of their conversation.

"So embarrassed . . . ," Mama signs. "You don't care how I feel."

"Listen . . . ," Papa signs, "Andrew Noble has insulted too many people, too many of our neighbors. And you calling innocent children 'mongrels.' What's come over you? I will not welcome him into our home again. Mary need never have known that the deaf are treated as less than human on the mainland. I have been soft with you. Now I must be strong for our family."

"Our family? Our family! You want to talk about our family? You don't understand . . . ," she signs. "Without George we have no family . . . I would have died for him . . ."

I am frozen in my place.

"Stop," Papa signs, raising his palm.

Mama signs, "I won't stop . . . You didn't love George as I did . . . You didn't . . ."

"Not true," Papa signs. "I grieve differently from you."

"What do you know of grief?" Mama asks cruelly.

Papa reaches for her, but she pulls away.

"You are not alone," Papa signs. "Be reasonable. You have me and Mary."

I hold my breath, terrified of what will come next.

"Mary was jealous of her brother . . . of how much he meant to me."

"No." Papa shakes his head.

My heart is breaking.

"Stop," Papa tells her firmly. "Stop. This is not only your pain."

Mama collapses onto the floor.

Silent.

Sobbing.

Papa bends down to hold her. She pushes him away. But he won't leave her side. When at last she stops fighting him, he cradles her in his arms.

I should go up to my room. But I can't.

I walk slowly toward Mama and Papa. I count ten steps, but it feels like a thousand.

When Papa helps Mama off the ground and into a chair, they see me. Mama's face is swollen from crying.

"I know," I sign, "I am not special like George . . . I know you loved him more . . . but I was never jealous . . . I was proud . . ." My words come out in stutters. "Memories . . . his death . . . I cannot escape . . . It was my fault he was in the road . . . Just a stupid game . . . I'm sorry, I'm sorry, I'm sorry . . ."

Mama looks at me like she's seeing me for the first time in nine months. I cannot read the expression on her face. It seems a mixture of anger, confusion, and, I hope, love. I raise my hands to beg forgiveness, but

I can't make words. I wish she could feel my heart and see the pain inside me.

Through my tears, I see Papa is looking at Mama. Still by her side. Waiting.

"I need time to think" is all Mama signs.

Papa touches Mama's shoulder, then lifts me in his arms and carries me upstairs. He helps me off with my gown and shoes. He puts me on my bed and covers me with a blanket.

"I knew, in my own way," he signs. "I saw my two children run out of the barn together. You were punishing yourself enough. Accidents happen. We can't always make sense of them."

I look downward. Papa takes my chin in his hand.

"She will see reason. Each of us has been blaming ourselves. I know you won't understand that now."

I manage to shake my head.

"Sleep," he signs, putting his hands under his head like a pillow.

He feels the question inside of me.

"Take care Mama," he signs. "Talk to Reverend Lee about Andrew Noble. Don't worry. It will be fine."

I can't imagine my family will ever be fine, but I want to believe Papa.

I fear the night, with its shadows and dreams.

I fear the morning, facing Mama in the light.

Chapter Nineteen

I pace back and forth in my bedroom. I feel the cold floorboards under the soles of my feet and stop to stare into the looking glass Grandmother Lila gave me. My hair is no longer the color of sunlight, and my hazel eyes look gray. Everything has dimmed.

I try to speak. My mouth twists up into a grimace, and my tongue flaps. It hurts my jaw to try to say words correctly. I squeeze hot tears out of my eyes. In the dream world, I have forgotten sign language. I can't scream, and I can't signal for help.

I awake suddenly, lying on my back. I pull my hands out from under my bedcovers. I wipe tears from my eyes and cheeks on a corner of the blanket. I lift my hands in the air, to make sure I have regained my ability to sign.

I sign my name, and a few words, like "house," "eat," "cat," and "wind."

My bedroom is near dark. From the color of the light, I guess the dawn will not come for another half an hour. I am not ready to encounter Mama. Will she yell at me with words I cannot understand? Will she turn her back and refuse to read my signs?

I quickly splash yesterday's water on my face, fasten stays over my shift, and dress in my gown, stockings, and shoes. I go downstairs as quietly as I can. I look to the back of the house. The light from the kitchen hearth has the dimness of night upon it. No one has gotten up to feed the fire.

As soon as I enter the yard, I see bright flashes from the Gay Head Light to the west. I picture the keeper igniting the spider lamp inside the tower's lighting room. I imagine him and me as lonely twins.

The barn doors aren't open. No sheep huddle by the stone wall. Though I catch sight of Bayard, running through the yard. How did he get loose? Why is he running in circles? Will Thomas or Eamon come tend to him? I know I can't contain him, so I continue my walk up the high road. I try to put last night out of my mind by creating a new story.

A fairy lived in a garden. She was so small she slept in a rose and collected its dew to drink. One day, a fly came to her rose and wanted to live in the crimson flower with her. She was not a selfish fairy, so she agreed to share the rose with the fly.

Soon the petals of the rose began to fall off. The fly didn't mind. He darted in and out of the rose with other flies. But the fairy became sick. She had to find another place to live. It was nearly winter, and the other flowers were freezing and dying on the vine. What could the fairy do?

I am startled out of my reverie when I see Andrew walking ahead of me, black satchel and carpet bag in hand. He is walking with a steady stride. His shoulders are bunched up. What reason does he have to be outside at this early hour?

Is he leaving? Good riddance!

As I watch him fade ahead, I remember George's book with my map of memories inside of it! Has Andrew absconded with it?

He turns off the high road. He must be heading for his schooner. I quicken my pace to catch up to him.

I trip over some rocks in the lane. Andrew turns around. He shouts at me and waves me away.

I walk closer to him. I start to sign, asking him about the book. I make the sign for "book," again and again. I put my hands together and repeatedly open and close them, hoping to get through to him.

It is an obvious sign; anyone who cares would guess its meaning. He puts down his bags and flaps his hands to mock my language.

"Never come back!" I sign to him. "Everything that comes from you is ugly." Even without knowing the words, it's obvious I'm not signing a friendly farewell.

Andrew speaks to me rapidly. His face in a cold rage, he laughs a mirthless laugh. Is he making fun of the fact that I can't understand his harsh speech?

The dawn is coming. I must return home before Mama and Papa find me missing. But not without my map.

I head toward the black satchel on the ground. I work the latch to open it. I quickly take out the samples in phials and notes on top. Some of them blow away. Furiously, Andrew chases the papers as I dig deeper for the book.

Before I find it, he strikes my hand and snatches the bag. He is still talking at me.

I pick up my pace on the lane to the high road, but I can feel Andrew follow me. What is he doing?

I look back. He stops when I stop. When I walk faster, so does he. Is he aiming to frighten me, or does he mean me harm?

Fortunately, Ezra Brewer's house is nearby. I'll climb through the window. I'll rouse him if he's not already awake. He has a musket and a Flintlock gun. He will not hesitate to offer me protection.

I break into a run. Andrew surprises me by giving chase.

Wet sand slows my pace. My shoes stick, the ground sucking at them. I feel as if I am trying to run through water.

I can see Ezra Brewer's house in the distance, smoke coming from the chimney. He is awake! Is he in his wicker chair? I raise my arms, waving wildly, hoping against hope that he spies me. My heart is pounding in my throat.

Andrew's long legs carry him quickly.

The sun is rising. It distracts me for a moment. I trip and fall on my stomach. I bite my lip as my chin hits the ground, bloodying my mouth and rattling my whole head.

I scrabble in the sand, trying to push myself up. It

sticks in my fingernails and slips under my feet as I try to get my legs under me once more.

Andrew is upon me. He grabs my hair and drags me backward across the sand toward his boat. My head feels like it's on fire. I struggle and kick, making it as difficult as possible for him to keep hold of me.

He is puffing hard. When he pauses to catch his breath, I reach up and scratch his hands with my sandy fingernails. He lets go of my hair, though some of it remains tangled in his fingers, and spits words from his lips.

I get up and find one last burst of energy in my legs. I run. I am close enough that I can see the lobster traps stacked ramshackle beside Ezra Brewer's shack and smell the wood smoke from his stove. I am nearly there when Andrew jumps on my back and takes me down with a thump. I scream. He puts his hand over my mouth. I try to bite him, but he avoids my teeth. I kick him as hard as my aching legs can manage, but it's no use.

He drags me to my feet with a grip so tight, I cannot extract myself. He pulls and pulls. I feel like he will tear me apart. I whip back and forth, trying to break free.

When we reach his bags, he stops. I am in too much pain to continue to fight.

With one hand, he removes the handkerchief from his breast pocket and a bottle from his satchel. He frees the cork with his teeth, soaking the handkerchief with its contents. He places it over my nose and mouth. What is it? I hold my breath for as long as I can. I do not want to breathe in whatever unction it is. But I am winded from the chase and need air.

I see gulls whirling above me. I see faded colors. I see foggy shapes. I feel like I am soaked to the skin from a rainstorm. I feel too heavy to resist anymore.

Part
Two

Chapter Twenty

I awake with my feet and hands tied together. The world around me slowly comes into focus. I see sails. Andrew Noble is standing over me. He looks calm as he navigates his schooner.

I have been tossed among the ship's tackle on deck. I gasp for breath and try to sit up.

I have never felt so helpless. I cannot even ask a question. He took my voice when he tied my hands.

I am freezing cold, my face chapped by the wind and sea spray. My mouth is as dry as an old rag. I open it and make a loud grunt and a whining noise. I sometimes do that if I am feeling ill in my bed so Mama will come up to check on me. Andrew Noble ignores me.

I grunt more and point with my chin to a jug by his feet. He lets go of the *Defiance*'s wheel, opens the jug, and holds it to my lips. He talks at me with a sour face, then quickly snatches away the jug.

He drags me across the deck, splintering an exposed

foot, and shoves me down below to a small cabin, which is nearly bare. There he unties me and locks the door. I shake the latch vigorously, but it won't open.

I pound on the door, again and again, until my knuckles are bloody. I lay my head against it, breathing heavily. I try to whine, pushing air out of my mouth. I can't do it. I try again, holding my fingers to my vocal cords to see if I can muster a sound loud enough to call for his attention. I work it up from my stomach into my chest into my mouth till it's an animal cry.

Andrew quickly opens the door. Upon seeing that I am in the state he left me, he sneers. He is carrying a bucket of water. I make the sign for "paper" and "writing." He tilts his head back in scorn and pours half the bucket on the floor. He laughs when I fall down to reach for it as it spills away.

I rinse the blood from my hands and my lip where it is swollen from our fight on the beach. I rub my wrists where they were tied. My hands, once filled with stories and conversation, are swollen and wordless.

I sit and close my eyes, trying to imagine myself anywhere but in Andrew's hold. I picture the stone wall along the high road in Chilmark, a familiar, solid path I know well. It helps to slow my tremors.

What are Andrew's intentions?

It would have been easy to kill me on the beach. He could have slipped me under the waves while I was unconscious. Why didn't he?

Then I remember some of the letter I read when I sneaked into the parsonage.

Bring back samples and acquire a live specimen.

I take mental stock of the items Andrew took from the Vineyard. There are several wax-sealed jars of well water, samples of Chilmark soil, clay, bark, and dung in bottles and phials. Does he have the genealogy Ezra Brewer wrote for him or the interviews with willing residents? And he took me. I am the live specimen!

My mind races with frightful ideas and questions.

Is he taking me to an asylum? What will they do to me? Will Andrew experiment on me?

Will I ever see my island again?

I remove my cloak and lay it over the stains on the hammock. Lying on it, I sob. My body spasms, and I dry heave.

I cast my mind back to my last night at home.

I imagine Mama and Papa consoling each other before falling asleep in each other's arms. I see them climbing the stairs to my bedroom when I didn't come down for breakfast. When they found my bedroom empty, did they search the barn and outbuildings? Did they run through the pasture? Did they hitch the cart and ride to Ezra Brewer's and the Skiffe house? Did they notice Andrew's schooner gone from the beach?

How will they ever find me?

Other thoughts creep in. I remember Mama's expression when I confessed my part in George's death. Does she forgive me now, or is she glad I'm gone? Papa knew. He'd guessed. Why didn't he talk to me and relieve my burden?

I cannot get away from my thoughts.

I try to focus on the moon glow that filters through the portal. It gives no warmth. A sea shanty Ezra Brewer taught me comes to mind. I slowly sign what I remember, feeling coming back into my hands.

Oh, have you heard the news, me Johnny?
One more day
We're homeward bound tomorrow

One more day
Only one more day, me Johnny
One more day . . .

How many days and nights will go on like this?
Will I ever again be homeward bound?

Chapter Twenty-One

By my count, ten days pass. I mark each day with a corn kernel from a sack of meal, with weevils, that I found in the corner.

Andrew shares his porridge. I try to sleep, often clutching my stomach. I cannot be sure if I have sea sickness or food poisoning. I feel I have lost weight. I empty my chamber pot out the portal, but sometimes the wind blows it back in. The room reeks like an unkempt stable. I struggle to keep my wits, let alone retain the bearing of a young lady.

Andrew brings me cold seawater to wash with, separate from the murky jug of drinking water. It stings against my cuts and bruises. What hurts worse is that he doesn't see me as someone created in the Almighty's image. I am a specimen, not a person. He never took an interest in island sign language, just our "infirmity." He could write to me, break my solitude with conversation, but he won't lower himself.

To comfort myself, I try to make up a new story

about a girl walking in a thick fog, looking for her lost dog. She calls to him with a long whistle, but he is wounded and barking. How will she ever find him?

I am too sad to finish.

Please Lord, never let me forget Reverend Lee's sympathy and the admiration that Miss Hammond showed me.

On the eleventh day, Andrew unlocks my door. Scowling, he passes me a handwritten note in neat script.

Rules
1. You agree to my explanation that you willingly left your home to travel with me.
2. You agree to be a willing subject of my study of your infirmity.

I look up at Andrew and shake my head. With his jaw set firmly, he points a long index finger at the letter. He wants me to continue reading.

3. You will always behave well and proper.
4. You will not run away.
5. You will not communicate with anyone away from my influence.

Break any of these rules and you will never again see your parents.

My heart sinks. I nod to show Andrew I agree to his terms. But behind my back, I cross my fingers.

He hands me a jug of clean water and indicates that I should wash my face and hands. I must clean off the dried blood, but I can hardly bear to pour water over my bluish skin. Andrew stands and waits. I dust off my cloak, untangle my hair with my fingers as best I can, and straighten my hat.

He gives me a hard look and points, ordering me on deck. After the darkness of my journey, I must squint into the morning sun. The freezing wind combs my still-tangled hair. My knees knock, and I long for the clean, warm blanket that Mama made me. At least the sea air smells better than my pigsty below.

I recognize Boston Harbor from plates in George's books. I have always dreamt of coming to see the place where the Revolution began but never like this.

The Inner Harbor is much bigger and busier than Edgartown Harbor. There are wharfs spread out on every side. I see a forest of ships' masts, like bare trees.

Side to side, we are surrounded by huge trading ships. I observe men loading heavy pallets with barrels and sacks, straining to lift them with ropes and pulleys onto the dock. Miss Hammond told us that sailors travel all the way from China to sell their goods.

I see a small monkey climbing the ropes on one ship. It has a chain on its leg. Andrew tethered me to the schooner with a rope around my right ankle as soon as he dropped anchor.

The sailors disembarking tall ships don't look like Ezra Brewer. They are young and thick with muscle, wearing neckerchiefs and striped shirts. They make fast business taking the sails down and unloading their various goods before they disappear in raucous groups into the city.

Could I escape Andrew and get lost among the sailors? But what would I do from there?

It is such a strange sight to see everyone around me flapping their lips but never raising their hands to communicate with signs.

There is so much to look at that the details overwhelm me and make my head hurt.

After Andrew finishes securing the schooner, he

unties my ankle. In a masquerade of chivalry, he takes my hand and helps me onto the dock.

Bostonians are bustling to and fro. Men rush around in breeches, tricorne hats, and shoes with brass buckles. Some even wear wigs.

Mama would look plain among the Boston ladies.

I admire their fine coats. Unlike our clothes, they are not all made from wool, cotton, and animal skins. I see many silk coats and even silk shoes, decorative hats with lots of lace and ribbons and plumes. I never could have imagined such finery.

I see a few freedmen, but I do not see any men I recognize as Wampanoag. They may be both, like Thomas. Ezra Brewer said slave catchers are plentiful in the city, and even free blacks are kidnapped and sold. The thought sickens me.

I am expected to carry Andrew's carpetbag. He holds tight to his black satchel with one hand. His other hand firmly grasps my upper arm as we weave through the crowd. My eyes water, but I won't cry out.

Flat brick buildings line the street, tall and close together. They wear no gabled roofs or other accents; their faces are flat with many windows like glaring

160

eyes. The cobblestones beneath my feet are worn smooth, though I still stumble in this unfamiliar place.

We pass North Church. I recognize it from the tall white steeple, a needle that almost pierces the sky. I imagine Paul Revere telling his conspirators to hang lanterns in the steeple to warn patriots about the movement of the British Army. Miss Hammond enacted his speech: "I alarmed almost every house, until I got to Lexington."

The streets grow narrower, dirtier. Beggars crouch in corners under worn blankets. I think of what Andrew said about deaf people begging for alms in the street. Are some of the people I see now deaf? If they are, would they understand my signs? Maybe the deaf of the city have no language.

Andrew seems to find them repugnant. Ezra Brewer told me that after the War for Independence, veterans who had lost limbs or were disfigured were treated as heroes. But I see no evidence that those with physical differences are respected.

As we turn a corner, a group of sailors burst from a tavern. One of them, burly with a bald head, tosses coin money in the air and catches it. The others laugh and nod.

Along another street, women stand in doorways. They are not elegant, like the ladies we passed at the wharf. They are dressed garishly, with too much face paint. They look at us and laugh.

Do they think I'm Andrew Noble's young bride? I want to call to them for help. I raise my hands to sign but quickly put them down before Andrew sees.

We stop in front of a dingy redbrick building on a narrow backstreet. I inhale foul odors. Are chamber pots dumped in the streets? I try not to retch.

A wooden sign swings over the doorway. It reads *The High Tide Inn*. Andrew lifts the heavy brass door knocker. A short, stocky woman opens the door, her face round with rheumy blue eyes and lemon-colored hair. She is not unpleasant-looking, just rough. She wipes her hands on her apron and embraces Andrew. He cringes at her touch, but she doesn't seem to notice.

They exchange words, with glances in my direction. I wonder in frustration what they are saying.

I bend my knee and sign, "How do?"

She looks me up and down and shakes her head, then leads us into the parlor and takes Andrew's coat before she rushes off. The parlor is tidy, though the furniture is threadbare, and the curtains are sooty.

Next to the parlor is a staircase. I wonder how many rooms are upstairs. I glimpse one young gentleman, slight of build with thin blond hair, who looks faintly respectable. He wears spectacles that slip down his nose, and his eyes narrow over the tops of the rims. I name him Mr. Squints. He almost bumps into me as he exits the parlor with a stack of books under his arm. I imagine he's a student.

The woman comes back carrying a tray with tea and meat stew, which she serves to Andrew. She signals me to the kitchen, and I follow.

It is cramped and dirtier than Mama's kitchen. The bricks are burnt black around the open hearth, and the room holds a heat that makes me sweat unpleasantly, even after the cold outside. There is no charm, not a piece of sea glass or a basket of dried flowers. Chairs are draped with laundry, and the table is piled with pots, pans, and assorted sundries. A rancid odor fills the room.

The woman gives the stew a stir, then walks over to

me. Looking me up and down, she pulls off my wool cloak and examines it. Then she takes my hands in hers and turns them over and over. She checks behind my ears and smells my person. I am rank from my travels.

I feel invisible.

I stare at the fire and only look up when I feel a strong vibration from the floor.

She's stomping her foot. She claps her hands in front of my face, then grabs my arm and leads me to the wash bin.

"Mary need never have known that the deaf are treated as less than human on the mainland," Papa had signed to Mama.

Is this how the world is outside of Chilmark? Is that why he doesn't like to travel off-island? Is it the reason Ezra Brewer mocks people and their morals? Have I been living on a cloud for eleven years? I look at the landlady as she talks at me. It's like I'm gazing into a looking glass and believing that the reversed reflection is the truth. I don't know what she wants.

Slam! My neck suddenly twists, and my head swerves to the left.

The landlady hit my right ear with the palm of her hand. I have heard of adults boxing children's ears. It creates a painful sensation, maybe even a ringing in my head, which is the closest I've come to hearing.

I put my hands on my knees and take deep breaths, then totter and stand up.

Grandmother Harmony, who became hard of hearing in her dotage, was able to read words on people's lips. When I was little, I tried it but found it impossible. I think I must attempt it again. If I can recognize even a handful of words, perhaps she will not be so rough with me.

Finally, the landlady makes motions like she's washing the dishes, points at me, and then to a stack of dishes. The way the scraps are stuck to them, I'd say they've been there for a few days. I wash them with a stained cloth in a bin of dingy, lukewarm water. When I finish drying them on a greasy apron, I am given a hard biscuit, which I sop in some of the lard left in the bottom of the kettle. I am not offered a seat, so I stand while I eat.

When I am done eating, the landlady takes me by the arm and leads me down a spiral staircase and through a narrow hallway. She stops, gives me the candle she was carrying, and gestures for me to go into a small room with a bed, a washstand, and a worn rug of indiscernible color. It is not nearly as bad as the schooner cabin.

I feel a quick bang. When I turn around, the landlady has vanished. I try the door, but she locked me in.

As I undress for bed, I remember the gold coin that Mama sewed into the hem of my gown for good luck. It is gone. I shudder to think Andrew took it while I was unconscious. I feel its loss as a prick to my skin.

My heart burns.

I don't have a story or a shanty in me tonight.

I cannot bear to think how distraught Mama and Papa must be. I should never have confronted Andrew. Sometimes I feel I can do nothing right.

I get down on my knees to pray. I remember a benediction from Reverend Lee.

I sign, "Our Lord, there is nothing in this life that is a surprise to You. You see our daily struggles and give us strength to endure through the power of Your Spirit. Create in us clean hearts and help us to remember that our strength comes from You alone. Amen."

Chapter Twenty-Two

By my rough estimation, it's been at least three weeks since I was stolen from my rightful place in Chilmark, almost two weeks traveling and eight days of monotonous chores at the inn.

I miss Mama's cranberry muffins. The way she spoons the batter so that each muffin contains the same amount of fruit. I miss waking up and going to the kitchen in my mobcap and shawl to see what Mama's baking. I close my eyes for a moment and imagine her looking up from kneading dough in the warm light of the hearth.

If I ever complained about helping Mama with chores, strike me down.

Most of the time, I am kept in the kitchen. The smells from boiled beef and cabbage permeate my clothing and hair. Living on an island and eating fresh shellfish and cod daily, I never knew why people complained of a fishy odor until I tasted one of the landlady's fish pies. She keeps it sitting too long. The rolls she bakes daily mitigate the smell. I call her Mrs. Muffins. Despite the charming name, I cringe every time she raises her hand. I never know what will set her off. Does she imagine she can unblock my ears by boxing them?

Ever since we arrived in Boston, I haven't been able to make up a story. Dreams no longer bother my sleep. I am too exhausted from housework. I remember nothing in the morning. Is this how Helen and Sally feel working in homes like the Skiffes? How do they keep up good cheer?

I haven't washed my gown and shift since I arrived, and my stench offends even me. I am grateful my room does not contain a looking glass.

When I'm not in the kitchen, I dust. Due to the open fires, dust is everywhere. I use a chamois cloth, and then shake it out. When the cloth is too dirty, I put it in the laundry bag. When we have a pile of dirty cloths and bedsheets, we wash them. The chores never end.

Today when I finish dusting, Mrs. Muffins has me bring Andrew a mug of warm rum. As usual, he is in the parlor writing, a sealed jar of Chilmark water next to him on the table. He looks me up and down with cruel disgust.

My fears that he would examine my person have not come to pass. Was I brought as a live specimen for his correspondent? Who is this person? When will he appear?

When Andrew drops some of his papers and I stoop to pick them up, he kicks my backside. Bruises already bloom on my arms and ribs from the pinches and jabs he subjects me to whenever he moves past.

In the kitchen, while we wash bedsheets, Mrs. Muffins hands me the bucket for more hot water. I watch her mouth to understand the words for "hot" and "water." I can almost recognize them. Then she starts talking about something unrelated, and I'm lost again. She talks constantly.

I remember seeing Ezra Brewer standing on top of a cliff on a windy day, signing with broad strokes to fishermen on the beach below. He asked them how many fish they'd caught. It is so easy to understand each other with signs.

When Mrs. Muffins wants me out of the way—to go out on errands, or if I've accidentally burned a tray of rolls—she locks me in my room for hours.

I had hoped Mama, Papa, and Ezra Brewer would have rescued me by this time.

What if they never find me? If only I could steal rag paper, a quill pen, and ink from Andrew's room, I could implore Mrs. Muffins for help. But I fear she is loyal to Andrew. I've noticed she keeps her ledger close by at all times, going over her accounts. Or else she locks it in a desk in the parlor. It would be near impossible to lay my hands on it. The boarder Mr. Squints may be my only hope.

When I have a moment free from chores, I watch him around a corner. He catches my eye and nods in a friendly fashion. He seems curious. At first, Andrew doesn't notice that Mr. Squints is genial toward me. I know that this will not last long. And Mrs. Muffins keeps me so busy with chores, I have nary a moment to myself to try to figure out how to communicate with him. If I seem distressed, will he try to help me? Or will he go to Andrew or Mrs. Muffins out of good but mistaken will?

I must discover his intentions.

Serving porridge and rolls with tea one morning, I linger in the dining room. The space is cramped, six chairs at a round table and a sideboard loaded with chipped dishes and cups. A grimy etching of the harbor hangs on the wall. I take my time finding a trivet to lay under the teapot.

I feel a low din. When I look up, I see Andrew laughing. He has two tin plates in his hands. I guess he banged them together to mock my deafness.

I quickly glance at Mr. Squints. He looks at Andrew with visible disgust. When he meets my eyes, his face reddens.

He knows I am deaf, and he is upset to see me disgraced. Thank you, Lord Almighty!

I hope to leave him a note in his bedroom when I make his bed, but if he has paper and a pen, I do not find them, and I must finish my task quickly before Mrs. Muffins boxes my ears. They have become so sore, I sleep on my back.

When I go to tidy the parlor before bed, I see a Bible left open on the table. I pick it up and read Proverbs 31:8–9: "Open your mouth for the mute, for the rights of all who are destitute. Open your mouth, judge righteously, defend the rights of the poor and needy."

Reverend Lee wouldn't view all deaf people as destitute and presume to speak for us. He wouldn't see muteness as the absence of oral speech but rather the condition of those who feel lost and unheard.

I wonder if this is a message from Mr. Squints! If he is interested in the rights of the poor and needy, maybe he will help me.

Chapter Twenty-Three

Today, when I finish sweeping and emptying the chamber pots, Mrs. Muffins gestures for me to take off my apron and put on my cloak and hat. We are leaving the inn? Andrew has gone out this morning, carrying his black satchel. He must not know because he would never approve.

What will he do if he finds out?

Mrs. Muffins doesn't tie my hands. Instead she gives me a woven white oak basket to carry. She carries a larger one. I follow her through the narrow streets covered in slush. My feet are blocks of ice. I wonder if I could find my way back to the wharf. Could I explain my predicament in pantomime to one of the sailors or a lady or a gentleman?

I pause in front of a large brick building and catch sight of my reflection in a window. Is that really me? I look like a vulgar beggar. A deaf and dumb one at that. If I desperately grabbed someone's coat sleeve, he'd surely hand me a ha'penny and shake me off.

The streets are crowded. The air is crisp. I can see my breath like smoke. Mrs. Muffins's pace is brisk. I hurry to keep up.

The streets are littered with rotten food and feces, not just horse flops. I see a lone sparrow. How do birds find food and water in this brick landscape? And where do they build their nests?

Abruptly, Mrs. Muffins puts her arm across my chest as a horse and cart fly around a corner. The horse bells remind me that Christmas is nearly upon us. Mama always made the holiday special for George and me. I can almost smell the fragrant pine boughs George and Papa placed on the mantelpiece in our sitting room.

Mrs. Muffins shakes me out of my thoughts. She points at our destination, Faneuil Hall. I know it from pictures George showed me. It's a long, two-story brick building with large windows facing north, south, east, and west. I look for the weather vane that Ezra Brewer once described to me, a golden grasshopper that sits on a large cupola. I see it!

Inside the hall are stands with men and women selling fish, meats, produce, and cloth. I watch them hawk their wares to passersby. I can feel the hum of the large crowd around me as I am pulled along. I watch person after person and try to make eye contact. Are they too busy to perceive my terrified state? I am desperate to see someone I know from home.

I wonder if Ezra Brewer knows any of the sailors. Very often the same sailors and traders go from the Vineyard to Boston and back again, over and over. Might they be keeping an eye out for a girl described like me? I try not to raise my hopes.

We stop at a fishmonger, and for a moment, I forget where I am. I turn to Mrs. Muffins and talk in signs. Her face reddens, and she quickly lowers my hands. The fishmonger looks at me like I'm half-witted. Am I? What if I can never again speak to someone in my own language?

I fear I might go mad.

Chapter Twenty-Four

We carry the heavy baskets back through the busy streets. I have the peculiar sensation that I am being followed. I slow my pace and glance behind me several times. I see a man turn his back to me. Farther along, the same man ducks into a doorway. I am so weary it may just be my imaginings.

Jeremiah Skiffe lives in Boston. Even though I am not sure I can ever forgive him, I would run to embrace him if we passed on the street. It's odd how an antagonist back home could be a welcome friend elsewhere.

I assist Mrs. Muffins putting away the groceries in the butt'ry. Andrew isn't in the parlor or the kitchen. Is he in his room? Is Mr. Squints in his?

Mrs. Muffins throws feed to the hens in the yard. I notice she left her ledger unattended on the table. While she has her back turned, I hastily cover it with a basket of dirty laundry. If I could tear out a page without being noticed, I could write a note to Mr. Squints! I need to find a quill.

Before I can scheme, I am pulled roughly toward the hearth and handed a bucket. Mrs. Muffins points at the kettle. She wants me to fetch water from the pump in the yard to stretch the oyster soup for another meal.

The laundry basket is still covering the ledger. But for how long? Mrs. Muffins will want to list our purchases.

In the yard, the hens crowd me. I'll bet she is stingy in feeding them too. Does she ever clean up their droppings? I'm surprised she hasn't had me do it. Their feet and now mine are covered in waste. There is a high fence, which the fowl and I would find challenging to escape.

Reentering the kitchen with a heavy bucket of water, I see the laundry basket is still on the table, but Mrs. Muffins is nowhere in sight. I am certain she's gone searching for her ledger. I must make haste.

I carefully rip a page from the back of her ledger. I discover that her true name is Martha Cummings. Seeing no quills, I take a splinter of charred wood from the kitchen fire and steady my shaking hand as I begin to write. It is messy, and the words smudge badly. I am too occupied to notice vibrations, and my heart leaps out of my chest when Mrs. Muffins is suddenly behind me. She tries to snatch the paper from me. The note is not finished, but hopefully Mr. Squints will understand my plea: *Kidnapped. Please help me get home to*

I don't know where I find the strength, but I jab her stomach sharply with my elbow. And I'm off! I make it out of the kitchen and to the stair landing before she is upon me. I open my mouth to howl, but hard as I try, I can only huff.

Mrs. Muffins grabs the note and leaves me lying on the landing.

I scramble down the stairs, hoping to wrest the note from her hands and finish my task. I enter the kitchen too late. With a crooked smile, she crumples the note and throws it into the fire.

She is talking, clapping, and signaling for me to make haste and get supper ready, but all I can do is watch that piece of paper curl and burn in the flames.

Andrew must have come in because she rushes toward the parlor, gesturing vividly. I follow her, throwing up my hands, begging her to stop. She ignores me.

In the parlor, Andrew is frozen as he listens, his eyes narrowing on me.

When Mrs. Muffins leaves, he grabs my arm and shakes me. His teeth are clenched as he talks. Spittle lands on my cheek, and I wipe it away. He throws me down on the rug. I am too frightened to move.

I gather enough courage to raise my eyes and see him furiously scribbling on a piece of paper. He flings it in my face and waits with a tapping foot for me to retrieve it.

He has written:

Remember the rules.

He drags me down to the servants' quarters. I fear he and Mrs. Muffins will never let me out of the cramped room again. I pound the bed with my fists.

That night, I lie awake and cry cold tears. Mr. Squints must be curious why I don't serve at supper. I wonder what story they make up, and if he believes it.

I pray, "Dear Lord, why have You brought me to this place? No matter how much I suffer and how my faith is tested, I will never stop trying to get back to my family and friends. I have learned too much too fast about how the world treats anyone who is different. I have to learn their rules, if I am going to beat them."

If Nancy were with me, would her outlook change? Would she be bolder with her father and less prejudiced toward freedmen and the Wampanoag? The world is bigger than we ever imagined.

I spend the next morning pacing back and forth on the tiny rug. My mind is frantic, like a rat in a trap. How will I ever get home?

In the afternoon, Mrs. Muffins unlocks the door. She drags me up to the kitchen and gestures for me to take tea to Andrew in the parlor. What is going on?

As I approach with the tray, I see another man standing in the entryway.

Mrs. Muffins comes in and reaches out her hand, which the stranger takes. She pours them each a cup of tea and offers them popovers.

The man has broad shoulders and long legs. He wears a suit rather than a coat and breeches, and his graying, dark hair is smartly slicked back. He walks around me, obviously disgusted by my feral state. I'm surprised he doesn't hold his nose. But he doesn't dismiss me outright.

His hawklike eyes, brown with gold flecks, are fixated on me with great curiosity. Could this be the man who wrote the letter to Andrew?

When Mrs. Muffins brings my coat and hat, I cling to her. Does this man intend to take me away? As Eamon has said, "Better the devil you know than the devil you don't." I moan as Andrew pulls me away from her.

Before I can resist, the older gentleman sweeps me out the door and into a stately carriage.

Chapter Twenty-Five

Though the carriage is majestic, with velvet interior and cushions, I fear the livery driver is taking us to some dark and foreboding place. Even with the beaver fur I've been given to wrap around me, I shiver. The curtains are drawn, so I can't see where we're going.

Andrew and the gentleman talk in what looks like a polite manner. There isn't an easy intimacy between them, but they are cordial. The older man's eyes are penetrating; I name him Professor Hawk. Andrew eagerly opens his black satchel to show him his writings. Professor Hawk raises his hand to indicate patience and then pats Andrew on the shoulder.

Am I not a person, like them? Does Professor Hawk not observe my dilapidated condition, my terror?

Twenty minutes must pass before the carriage slows down and comes to a halt.

The driver holds open the door. I see a metal sign that reads *Beacon Hill*. Oil lamps light the streets. In

Chilmark, the high road is pitch-black at night, unless there is a rider with a lantern.

The building before me is four stories in height, with pilasters rising from the top of the first-story porch to the roof. It is so large it cannot possibly be someone's home. Is this an asylum?

I am led through the elegant foyer into a front room with a cold slab of a table and sharp instruments. When I turn back, I see the latch rattle. They've locked the door. Why must they always cage me like an animal?

My breath comes quicker as I examine the instruments. They resemble the tools hanging in our barn, only smaller, more refined, of smoother, polished metal.

My heart pounds.

The desk is loaded with papers. There is no attempt to conceal them. I spot quill pens and an inkwell. Do I risk defying Andrew so soon after my last transgression?

A framed document has the name Dr. Henry Minot. He must be the gentleman who brought me here. I wasn't far off calling him a professor. I wonder about his surname. Pronunciations of English words vex me. George sometimes made futile attempts to explain them to me.

I have never been examined by a formal doctor. Mama uses home remedies when we are sick. Teas and poultices made from hazelnut and sassafras bark. We are not the only settlers who use Wampanoag cures.

I see the handle of the door rattle. A thin girl wearing a white-and-gray gown enters the room. She looks to be about Andrew's age with a sharp face and shrewd eyes under a twist of fiery hair. She must be the doctor's housekeeper.

She has an open, curious look about her. She reminds me of Miss Hammond. I decide that her name is Miss Top because she seems to bob a half-curtsy every five steps and, when she turns, she turns almost fully as if she is spinning around. She never stops moving.

Rolling her hands from her knees up over her head, she pantomimes for me to undress. I know for certain that Mama wouldn't approve. I take off my cloak, hat, shoes, and stockings, and cross my arms. I refuse to go any further.

184

Miss Top shakes her head. Her lips are moving. She takes hold of my gown, loosening the ties on the bodice and then yanking down the skirt. At the inn, I was overworked and underfed. My muscles are strong, but I am too exhausted to resist. She instructs me to sit on the cold table. I shiver in only my undergarments.

Andrew and Dr. Minot enter the room. The doctor motions for Miss Top to light a fire in the woodstove. She does as asked and leaves me alone with them. Blood pounds in my head.

Dr. Minot looks at my ears. He looks in my mouth and feels the cords on my throat and the natural bumps on my head under my thick hair. He talks to Andrew, who takes a metal band like a crown and puts it round my head. He adjusts it with tiny screws. I jerk as if someone slapped me. I can feel a trickle of blood down my right temple. I raise my hand to wipe away the blood, but Andrew lowers it.

I feel like a bare tree in the wind, but I won't let myself cry.

Andrew removes the metal band. He measures its diameter and notes it in a book on the desk. I have the urge to spit in his face. What does the size of my head have to do with anything except fitting a new bonnet?

Miss Top returns while Andrew and Dr. Minot wash their hands in the fresh water she pours into a basin. They talk, turned away from me.

Before I know what's happening, Miss Top takes me by the wrist and pulls me up carpeted stairs and into a room with a tub larger than any I've seen. When she gestures toward the high water, I know she's asking me to climb in.

"No, no, no, no, no," I sign.

I will not be stripped bare by strangers. How am I to know that this girl won't attempt to drown me, like an unwanted litter of kittens?

The shift Mama sewed is not easily torn off. I cross my arms over my chest and will not cooperate. The girl persists in her duty. I pinch. I push. I kick. But again, she overpowers me and forces me into the water. I slip under and come up coughing. When she scrubs my hair and body, I wail and must sound like a banshee or an Irish spirit.

Miss Top's mouth pinches into a thin line as she

runs her fingers over my bruises. Papa allows his flock of sheep more privacy than I am being granted.

I am so filthy the water darkens quickly. Miss Top drains and refills the tub. By that time, I breathe easier. I even hold my breath and go underwater entirely. For a moment, I can pretend I am bathing in the fresh spring at home.

Miss Top sits on the floor, flushed and panting. She wipes the hair back from her forehead. Our struggle seems to have subdued her. For the moment, she is less efficient and more forgiving. She gives me a clean shift, a mobcap, and a shawl.

Miss Top leads me to a large room with a canopied four-poster bed. It is beautiful, like something out of my stories. The polished wood floor is covered with rugs fancier than our braided ones at home. Pretty combs, soft brushes, and a wreath of pine and berries sit on top of the bureau. I am not yet ready to glance at my reflection in the floor-length mirror.

Miss Top carries the green gown Mama made me with her arm outstretched. I start to protest. She seems to understand my attachment to it, no matter its wretched state. She lets me hold it to my clean cheek for a moment before she throws it in the fireplace. I grab the fire poker and try to retrieve it, but Miss Top snatches the poker and uses it to prod the gown and ensure it burns quickly. I drop to my knees.

Miss Top leaves. I rush to the door behind her. I can see her wiggle the latch to make sure it is secure. I noticed she keeps a ring of keys in her apron. Are there other prisoners here?

I pace the floor, still avoiding my reflection in the mirror. Behind the flowery drapes are two floor-to-ceiling windows. They are covered by iron bars. Why should there be bars on the third floor? Who else has been held here, and for how long? Where are they now?

I try in vain to shake the bars. My hands can barely reach the panes. I cannot smash them in the hope of escape.

I sit with my legs tucked under me on the duvet and brush out my hair. I wish Mama were here to gently work out the knots. I yelp as I snag them.

I should sleep peacefully in such a bed. But it is too large and empty. I curl into a ball. I have the quivers, so I pray where I am instead of getting down on my knees.

"Lord Almighty, I've always believed You listened to me and kept me safe. Please send someone to rescue me before they do me further harm. I will never again tell lies."

No one comes.

Chapter Twenty-Six

When Miss Top shakes me awake in the morning, I startle. I wonder if it is different for hearing people, who must come awake slowly to the sounds of morning. She smiles and nods. I wait for her to box my ears or drag me down to a waiting pile of unwashed dishes. So I am surprised when she pours fresh water into my basin, and more so when I am given a plate with oysters and hare. I eat quickly.

After stoking the fire and drawing the heavy drapes, Miss Top exits, and I get out of bed.

I feel no vibrations through these thick walls, nor through the floors with their heavy rugs. Occasionally, I sense a small shudder as a door is closed forcefully. Are others held here against their will? Are the cries of the insane all around me? I shiver and wrap my shawl tighter.

Miss Top enters again and, before I can peek into the hall, quickly closes and locks the door behind her. She lays new clothes on the bed. She looks at me boldly and holds up the petticoat. I decide not to struggle and allow myself to be outfitted in the red gown, complete with stays, matching shoes with paper inserts, and an elegant felt hat.

Why all this finery? It feels like a costume. From Andrew's written rules on the *Defiance*, I assume I will be poked and prodded by more cold hands, and who knows what else.

Miss Top looks behind her and quickly rushes out. She must have heard a sound beckoning her. She exits through a small gap between the door and doorframe. I see the handle rattle, to ensure it's locked.

I cross the room and look out the barred windows. Beacon Hill lives up to its name, as it is a hilly place, with stretches of land and trees. A fresh snow spreads out like a white blanket brushed to a fine nap. It must have been pasture land in the past. It resembles Chilmark more than anything I've seen in the city.

In the distance, I glimpse a massive structure made of brick with a huge golden dome. Not as picturesque as Faneuil Hall but equally impressive. I wonder if it is a grander version of our Meeting House.

Unlike Mrs. Muffins's, with its comings and

goings at all hours, Dr. Minot's street is distant and silent. I don't see many residents bustling to and fro. I have never experienced such physical isolation. Quiet within, quiet without.

I press my face between the bars imagining the details I cannot see. Are there trails of deer and other animal footprints?

It suddenly occurs to me that all I survey was once Indian land. Miss Hammond taught us the Massachusett Nation had many sachemships before the white settlers arrived. Outbreaks of small pox devastated their numbers. Does that mean this peaceful winter landscape also serves as a graveyard? Where are the survivors?

I turn back to the room and explore the bureau drawers. Inside are linens that would make Mrs. Skiffe burn with envy, so fine and smooth to the touch, impeccably ironed and folded. In the bottom drawer, carefully tucked under a sheet, I find a set of carved wooden toys. With delicate hands, I pick up Noah's Ark and think of Reverend Lee's sermon.

I run my hand along the bright yellow paint on a duck with wheels and its cord for pulling. Such fine wooden toys, made with great craftsmanship, are not meant to be hidden away in a drawer. I turn the duck over in my hands, and something falls into my lap. It is wrapped in a dainty handkerchief with the initials "A.M." sewn into it. Inside, I feel a flat oval the size of an egg. I unwrap it.

A cameo! I've rarely seen anything so elegant in my life. One side is ivory, painted with the cherubic likeness of a girl only a little younger than I am. She has rosy cheeks and a cloud of dark hair surrounding her face. I replace the cameo in the drawer. Did my clothes belong to this girl? Is the room hers too?

I think of how Mama keeps George's room as he left it. She would never let another soul occupy it.

Just then, the door flies open. Andrew seizes me by the arm and leads me toward the door. I lag behind but don't resist. The first two doors we pass are open. One of them is the water closet where I bathed. Another is a bedroom smaller than mine. It's bright and tidy. The rest of the third floor appears unoccupied. Perhaps this is not an asylum, after all.

If it is a personal residence, it is larger than the largest home on the island. Dr. Minot must be a very prestigious man. But if this is his home, where is his family?

We descend the curved staircase. When I realize I am being taken to the room with the cold table and the instruments, I dig in my heels. Andrew pulls me roughly by my elbow and shoves me ahead of him.

When we enter the front room, Dr. Minot seems taken aback. His sharp gaze softens, and I watch as he clasps his hands and wrings them. Is it the clothes?

He gestures for me to sit on the table. My legs swing nervously. Andrew stands to one side, his gaze warning me not to embarrass him.

Dr. Minot pushes against the roof of my mouth with his index and middle finger. It makes me gag, but I decide it would be unproductive to bite him. He follows my vocal cords down to my breast. I blush and look away. He moves two fingers back and forth in front of my eyes to see if I follow them. Then he moves my lips open and closed, open and closed, like a doll, and traces my jawline.

Miss Top busies herself with the woodstove but also watches us.

Dr. Minot bends down to look into my eyes. I try

to make my gaze as intelligent as possible. I search his face. After a few moments of mutual staring, he looks away.

He signals for me to stand and twirls two fingers on his right hand for me to turn around. He feels my back from my neck to my rear. What notions they have about our deafness! I face him and point to my ears to indicate *that* is my one peculiarity.

That makes him stroke his chin, and he seems to chuckle.

Andrew steps closer and talks rapidly. I imagine he is pompously interjecting his observations. Dr. Minot gestures and leads Andrew away.

Standing at the windows with his arms crossed, he calmly listens to Andrew, who in comparison appears like a rabid dog frothing at the mouth. The doctor lays his hand on Andrew's shoulder to steady him and speaks to him directly. I wish I knew what they were saying.

Miss Top leads me back to my room. Before ascending the stairs, I glance back at the front door. I must attempt to escape before I lose my wits. I am certain Mama and Papa are despairing, not knowing my fate.

Though Mama's words on my last night at home still haunt me.

With these thoughts and feelings worrying my mind, I fall into a fitful sleep. I don't know how many hours have passed when Miss Top returns with a slice of meat pie for supper. I sit up and gobble it quickly. As she stokes the hearth fire, she watches me. Our eyes meet, and she smiles.

I smile back. Might she help me?

She stands, and before she can leave, I make the sign for dipping a quill pen in an inkwell and writing on paper. She repeats my signs. But does she understand their meaning?

She smiles ruefully and shakes her head.

My heart sinks. Has Andrew told Dr. Minot that I am a half-wit, who is not to be trusted or believed?

There must be another way.

I try signing, "Please, please." My face shows my desperation. She repeats the signs and imitates something of my facial expression. Is she connecting the two as words? I sign, "I am stolen. I must return to my family." Again, she repeats it back to me. She nods and waits for me, but it's clear that she doesn't know what I've said. Deflated, I drop my hands.

Miss Top glances at a small bell hanging near the ceiling beside the bed. Someone must have rung it. She half curtsies and bobs, quickly exiting and locking the door behind her.

I wash my hands and face in the basin. I look out the windows and pray for some sign that I will one day be home again.

I swear I see a man in a cap staring up at the window. Is it only wishful thinking that he sees me?

Chapter Twenty-Seven

I must have fallen into a leaden sleep because Miss Top has already drawn the drapes and left a tray with porridge and syrup by the time I wake. I cross the room and peer anxiously out the window. No one looks up at me. Perhaps I only dreamt the man.

Desperate for some way out of here, I turn over every object in the room. Most of them are elegant but useless. I find the cameo and cradle it in my hands. I wonder what the girl's name was. Did she live only to the age in the picture? Does her body lie under the snowy hills or in a family plot far away? Why was I never brave enough to visit George's grave?

When I feel the door rattle, I quickly stow the cameo back in the drawer. Miss Top has come for my breakfast tray. This time she stays and prompts me to sign by repeating the words she's memorized and then pointing at me. I attempt to expand her repertoire, to make her see the gravity of my situation.

My signing is slow and exaggerated. Again, I make

the sign for "writing," with raised eyebrows, asking for a pen and paper. Once again, she shakes her head. This time it occurs to me that she may be illiterate. Or has Andrew forbidden her to give me anything but food?

We create a game where I point to things in the room and make their signs. She catches on quickly. Soon I am running back and forth between the objects, and she is making the signs. We exchange roles, so she can point, and I sign.

Then I string words together. I combine "bed" for my Vineyard home with "rain" outside the window, while rocking on my feet, holding my breath, and clutching my stomach as if I am about to be sick. I am trying to indicate my passage on the *Defiance*. Miss Top looks delighted by my performance.

I collapse on the floor. How will we ever understand each other?

The bell must call her away again because she waves goodbye and vanishes behind the door. I noticed that she doesn't rattle the handle. Has she been careless or is her trust in me growing? Do I dare cross the threshold?

Out the window, I see Andrew walk away from the

house. He has a steady stride and his shoulders are bunched up, just as he looked on the beach my last day on the Vineyard. His discontent worries me. If Dr. Minot is not supportive of his theories, Andrew may take me elsewhere.

This is my chance! I don't feel any movement or vibrations in the house. Quietly, I creep downstairs to the front door. It is locked. I rattle the handle. I try to poke my smallest finger into the keyhole. I pray, "My Lord, open the door so I can flee and be brought to safety, like Moses in the bulrushes." It doesn't budge.

I tiptoe to Dr. Minot's office. Thankfully, he is not there, and Miss Top is nowhere to be seen either.

I sift through the massive pile of papers on Dr. Minot's desk. It is untidier than I remember from my first night in the house. I recognize Andrew's handwriting on several letters.

I was careful to fish in the next town over and barely took a bite when I was invited for dinner in one of their island hovels, lest I be infected with the deafening element . . .

I set down the paper, feeling sickened. That's when I see, on a table in the middle of the room, George's geography book! I open it and find the map of memories still tucked safely inside. Each pen stroke is as familiar to me as the lines in my hand, distinctly George's creation and drawn with such love. I clutch it to my heart, feeling tears prickle behind my eyes, before I tuck it into the bodice of my frock.

In a red leather-bound notebook, I see the words *The girl is in good health.*

I read on:

I find no strange marks or deformity on her body. Her ears and tongue look as normal as those who can hear and speak. Her vocal cords feel no different and her skull is of normal size.

We have the deaf and dumb in Boston, of course. They aren't easy to find. The few I've encountered are quite dull. What interests me about this young girl is that she seems otherwise perfectly normal.

She looks sullen but not moronic. When she first came to us, she was in such a wretched state,

*practically an urchin, and I was reluctant to share
my beloved Amy's belongings with her. I have
kept them so long and so well.*

I remember the handkerchief concealing the cameo. It was embroidered "A.M." Amy Minot. My clothes and the other objects in the room must have been hers.

I get the feeling I'm being watched. I turn around, but no one is in the room. I continue reading:

*I wonder what kind of arrangement Andrew made
with her parents. He told me that her mother
was hospitable enough. The poor woman lost her
son in a horse-cart accident. He said her grief
made her daughter's upkeep too hard a burden to
bear. She was pleased to hear she may come to
some use in his scientific inquiry.*

Upkeep! I know I wasn't as useful as I might have been, but I was never a derelict. Whatever tensions came between Mama and me, I know she never thought me useless.

202

I continue reading:

But I fear that I have come to possess a few doubts about Andrew's story.

He told me that the deaf and dumb of Martha's Vineyard are congenital idiots, unintelligent and unlearned. Yet, he just showed me a comprehensive genealogy created by a deaf and dumb seaman. How could an idiot create such a thing? I wonder what other questionable conclusions he has drawn or mistruths he has told me?

Once again, I feel something. I face the door to the office but see no one.

Slowly, I turn to look out the window, and the hair on the back of my neck tingles. There *is* someone. He is wearing a Monmouth cap and looking in at me from the street! I pull back from the pane.

I can't help but look again. He is still there.

His cap is pulled down over his brow and ears. I haven't seen one of those since I left the Vineyard. Have my prayers been answered?

I look again. I dare to raise my hand in a wave. The man does the same!

Just then, I feel something on my shoulders.

I jump and a startled sound flies from me. I look up to face Dr. Minot, who is gazing at his journal in my hand.

Spinning round, I slip from his hold, drop the journal, and run upstairs. Without looking back, I close the bedroom door and sink to the floor.

My face is hot with unshed tears. I rock back and forth clutching the map.

Chapter Twenty-Eight

Has the man with the Monmouth cap come to rescue me? I look out the window, but there is no sign of him, only a group of merry wassailers or carolers. They are standing under an oil lamp, huddled together, and singing.

It must be Christmas Eve.

The flame I was keeping lit inside of me snuffs out.

I survived the journey to Boston in my own filth. I've swayed from hunger and had my ears boxed in Mrs. Muffins's kitchen. I've been stripped bare and examined. But now I feel broken. Darkness grows on the edges of my vision. Wave after wave of terror sweeps over me. I gasp for breath.

My hands make signs, and I don't know what I am saying. I am an observer in my own body.

I crawl over to the hearth rug and retch water. The fire doesn't warm me. I shake all over.

Lord, why hast thou forsaken me? Could we have been wrong on the island? Are deaf-mutes lower beings?

I find the strength to stand and stumble toward the looking glass. Holding on to the bureau, I lean into my reflection. Whose eyes are those? The cold stare of a dead fish, lucky to be no longer wriggling on the hook. The nose squashy and too big for the sunken cheeks. The mouth a scar.

I glimpse movement behind me; it is Miss Top. Why did she come?

I make my way to the bed. I look at the small orange on my pillow and choke back tears.

The first time I had an orange was last Christmas. A sailor gave it to Papa, and he gave it to me. I ate the juicy fruit, slice by slice, and kept the peel to flavor Mama's baking.

That same night, after supper, while George examined his new telescope with Mama, Papa drove me down to Ezra Brewer's house to deliver a pudding I helped Mama make. I also brought a small skein of wool as a toy for Smithy. Mama and I tied red velvet hair ribbons to give to Nancy and Miss Hammond. George had caught the goose. He had gone out hunting with Papa and Mr. Pye. The men slapped my brother on the back for bringing home the finest bird. I can nearly taste the delicious crisp skin we ate together, after thanking Our Lord for the bounty. The next day, we brought whatever was left over to the Meeting House for the less fortunate.

I must spend hours lost in my memories.

In the early dawn, I see Andrew leave again. Where is he going when it's still dark outside? I have to get out of here. I must communicate with Dr. Minot.

I rattle my door latch, but it is locked. There is no light through the keyhole. I peer into it and see the key was left in the other side of the door. I fetch the wrought-iron fire poker, slip the map of memories beneath the doorframe, and gently push the poker's pointed tip through the keyhole. Slowly, slowly, till the key drops on the map. I hope it didn't make a loud clank. I pull the map toward me and seize the key. The door unlocks easily.

I dress, tuck the map back into my bodice, and creep down the staircase. When I reach the ground floor, unfamiliar vibrations startle me.

I whip around. A large clock strikes five o'clock. Will the chimes wake the household?

The door to Dr. Minot's office is ajar. I run to the window but see no one.

The piles of papers on the doctor's desk have been tidied up. Paper, ink, and pounce sit beside the journal. I start reading where I left off:

Nora has canny instincts. She believes Mary is quick and responsive. But we shouldn't get too excited, or expect too much, from Mary. She may be dimwitted, after all.

Miss Top's true name is Nora.

I imagine that having a child like Mary could be a burden. But still I am curious what Andrew's agreement was with her parents. Was there some other incentive? Did he promise them a share in his fortune, if he ever makes his name? Did he buy her from them?

I agree with Andrew that the source of the affliction is truly mysterious. I am not sure I agree that it is caused by an impure element on the island. It will take a lot of work to prove his conclusion. I have told him I cannot sponsor him without more significant evidence.

His outburst of anger and talk of betrayal concern me. It explains why he didn't get along at Yale. He has a hard time accepting instruction or helpful criticism.

I carefully tear a page from the back of the journal. I pick up the quill pen and dip it in the inkwell. I often stumble when switching from signing to written English. This time, my words come as quickly as a rushing brook.

Sir,

I would like to disabuse you of certain notions. I did not leave the Vineyard willingly with Andrew Noble. My parents did not agree to let me travel with him. They certainly did not sell me to him as a curiosity! In my town, a girl like me is not considered to be a burden.

You wrote of Andrew's angry outbursts, so it will not surprise you that he kidnapped me. I wish to leave and be reunited with my family.

I have noticed a man outside the house. He dresses like the seamen I know on Martha's Vineyard. I am hoping he is part of a rescue plan by Vineyard residents. Whether or not you believe it, there are people who would search high and low to recover me.

I need your help. Though I am held hostage in your home, I bear no ill will against you. You have also been deceived.

Thank you for sharing your daughter Amy's beautiful possessions with me. As my friend Thomas once said, "The loss of a loved one is the hardest thing to bear."

If you are a man of honor, I trust you will assist me.

Yours truly,
Mary Lambert

As soon as I stop writing, I feel a door open and slam shut in the house. My heart pounds. The door to Dr. Minot's office slowly opens.

I look for a place to hide. Dr. Minot appears. He studies me with his sharp hawk eyes. In a panic, I drop the papers and run from the room, but I don't know where to go. I freeze in the front hall. I think Dr. Minot shouts after me. If I run up the stairs, I will be trapped.

My head feels light, and I feel myself fall.

Chapter Twenty-Nine

When I open my eyes, I am lying on the table in Dr. Minot's examination room, with a blanket over me. I feel hot and dizzy. I stir and moan. Nora rises from a nearby chair.

I quickly pat my body to make sure I am still dressed. That makes Nora laugh, in a friendly way. She stands up and hands me two written pages. My letter. I'm too nervous to meet her gaze.

Has Andrew returned to the house? Has Dr. Minot shown him what I wrote? What revenge will Andrew seek for the things I said about him?

I turn helplessly to Nora. She points to her eyes and then to the papers. It's Vineyard sign language for "read."

I see that the papers in my hands are not written in my scrawl.

Dear Mary,
Thank you for your letter. It's quite astonishing
to me that you can write English when you've

never heard the language spoken. I always thought that hearing was the most important sense. Perhaps I am wrong.

I have a predicament. I sympathize with Andrew's interest in discovering the cause of widespread deafness on Martha's Vineyard. It is a worthy pursuit. Though I don't agree with the scandalous way he went about it.

I won't call down the law on him. He is already estranged from his father, who is a friend and a respectable man in Greenwich, Connecticut. I don't wish to bring further disgrace upon their family.

The question is what to do with you. How do I explain to Andrew that I released you?

The sailor you wrote of has business at the harbor. I have spoken with him, and his intentions seem honorable. So here is my plan: When he appears outside the house, Nora will unlock the front door for you. You will run to meet him and then make your escape.

Andrew will be none the wiser. He might try to return to your island. But your townsfolk will

make sure he doesn't receive cooperation in his
research and can't steal you away again.

You have challenged my perceptions about the
deaf and dumb. I hope to see you again someday.
Nora is very interested in visiting your island, to
conduct her own research of your hand gestures.

You have brought fond memories of my Amy
back to me. I know she would want me to help
you return to your family.

Godspeed,
Dr. Henry Minot

I feel stunned. Dr. Minot believes me? And Nora
does too?

Hastily, I get my coat. Nora hands me some food
to travel with. We stand by the front window and keep
watch for the man in the Monmouth cap. I don't know
who is more anxious.

Nora raises her eyebrows and quickly points to a
passing sailor. I shake my head. I pace back and forth.
Nora wants to practice signing with me. I am agitated,
but I indulge her.

She is learning as quickly as a child. She points to

the window, the sky, the trees and birds. I make the signs and try to string them together in sentences with the signs she's already learned. It distracts me until Nora grips my arm. "There! There!" she signs, pointing her index finger.

A man is coming down the street. The snow obscures my view. Please let it be the man with the Monmouth cap.

In horror, I see that it is Andrew.

I run to the front door with Nora on my heels. She unlocks it quickly, and I dash out, without so much as a "thank you." I run in the opposite direction from Andrew. Panicked, I pray that the man in the Monmouth cap is not far, and that I can find him or another sailor before I am recaptured.

The brick cobblestone streets are icy. I slip a few times in my fancy shoes. A strong wind gusts off the harbor and down the streets. It twirls me around and almost knocks me down. I drop Nora's food package. My teeth chatter from cold and fear.

I sprint as best I can, panting like a workhorse. When I dare to look back, I catch sight of Andrew coming around a corner. His tall, thin frame is unmistakable. I feel the blood drain from my face. How did he find me? Did he threaten Nora?

I try to remember my way back to the wharf with landmarks, but I'm sure I'm off course. I run through throngs of Bostonians. There is enough bustling activity to shield me. No one seems to notice I'm being hunted.

I stop momentarily to catch my breath. That's when I feel a strong hand grab the back of my coat. I spin around, fearing I will collapse on the spot. But it isn't Andrew. It is the man with the Monmouth cap!

He is burly with blond curls. He looks me up and down and nods. I ask him his name. He shakes his head. He doesn't know sign language. Did he deceive Dr. Minot? Is he working with Andrew?

He grabs hold of my arm and rushes me along. I wrestle with him, and he looks surprised by my resistance. I try to bite his gloved hand, but he does not release me from his grip.

Behind me, I catch sight of Andrew again. His blue eyes seem to burn in their sockets, and his jaw is set. He can't be more than twenty feet from me.

I look up at the man with the Monmouth cap. He looks at me and follows my terrified stare. The man picks me up, and when I scream, he covers my mouth with his hand. He runs away from Andrew and deposits me on the dock. Again, I try to flee, but he pushes me backward, and I fall hard on my backside into a docked cutter. A grizzled man races toward me. Ezra Brewer! And it is not just any cutter. It is the SS *Black Dog*!

I collapse into Ezra Brewer's open arms. His embrace is strong and gentle at the same time. I close my eyes and rest my head on his shoulder, choking on my own sobs.

He releases me and signs "thank you" to the man, who tips his hat and disappears into the crowd on the wharf. Ezra Brewer jumps up and quickly works the rigging.

"Andrew is here," I sign.

"Saw him," he signs matter-of-factly. "We'd better get going."

While Ezra Brewer prepares the boat, I keep watch in case Andrew attempts to board the *Black Dog* before we leave Boston Harbor.

As we begin to sail out of the Inner Harbor, Ezra Brewer surveys me. I've never seen his dark blue eyes so worried. Do I really look that awful?

"Mary," he signs, with a twinkle in his eye, "I'm glad to see you, but I can't say I admire your frills and brass buttons. You're dressed a mite too fancy for the *Dog*."

A waterfall tumbles inside me.

Chapter Thirty

"I can talk in signs with you!"

"I believe that's what we're doing," Ezra Brewer responds.

"I haven't conversed with anyone in ages," I tell him.

"It's about time you did," he signs.

I look behind us and see the sails flying on the SS *Defiance*. Andrew must have been aiming to take me to his schooner, not back to Dr. Minot's. He must have left early to prepare it.

The *Black Dog* is a midsized cutter. The rig makes the boat faster and easier to maneuver than many larger boats. We stand more than a fair chance against Andrew's schooner.

Sailing into the Atlantic, the waters are choppy.

"Andrew is following us!" I sign.

"We'll sail south of Boston and then around Cape Cod," signs Ezra Brewer. "We'll stay on the sea to take the harder route." He winks. My stomach drops. The back Cape can be perilous to navigate, even with a capable captain at the helm. The *Mayflower* couldn't pass the Cape to sail on to the Colony of Virginia; they had to land on the tip of Cape Cod.

When we look back again, we see that Andrew has navigated a course straight toward us. "It will take him time to catch up," Ezra Brewer assures me. "We won't sail into swift currents for a while."

I raise my hands to sign again, but find I have nothing to say. In Boston, I thought if I ever saw anyone from the Vineyard, I would spill out all the details of my kidnapping. Now I can't bring myself to say them.

Ezra Brewer glances at me, waiting to see what I'll sign. I want to say something. Anything that's not about me.

He shakes his head. "A fool I've been! You'll be wanting food and water." He gives me a hard biscuit to nibble on.

"We are going home now," I sign.

"Indeed, the whole town has been trying to find you and making prayers for your safety. Your ma and pa were very hard hit." I notice he keeps one eye on the helm and the other on the schooner following us. His left hand reaches down for a bottle. There isn't one there, and he scowls.

"I don't want them to grieve anymore," I tell him. "We've been hurting long enough."

Ezra Brewer smiles broadly and signs, "You should know that curly headed gal has been sulking and sighing all over the island."

"Nancy?" I ask. I can't wait to embrace her again. I'm sure she's been bored without me. "How is she?"

He signs, "Doesn't help her father is carrying on about his land rights."

"Is Mr. Skiffe persisting?" I ask, shaking my head.

Ezra Brewer works his mouth and starts signing again. "You can count on that. He made a mess over a piece of land, just because he wanted it when he has enough. What sort of reason is that? I've got all I need with my boat and my cat."

Ezra Brewer looks at me, to make sure I am paying attention. I am watching him, though I can't help but glance back to see how close Andrew is. It's hard to tell if he is gaining on us.

"How about Thomas Richards?" I ask. "Is he still working the farm with Papa?"

"I daresay he is. And that colt of your brother's, Bayard, well, I should tell you that story. The morning that malefactor absconded with you, Bayard had his hackles up. He knew something was wrong."

I remember the horse running free in the yard.

Ezra Brewer continues. "Well, he jumped the fence and went after you. But he was so agitated that he got whipped and cut by bare branches running down the high road and never made it to you. He had a few deep wounds and one eye swollen shut when they found him."

"Oh no," I sign.

"I am not trying to make you feel sorry," he signs. "It's just because you mentioned Thomas. Can ye believe, it was that young daughter of his who helped nurse Bayard back to health? You know how finicky horses are; they only like who they like, and you can naught change their minds. He wouldn't let the Irishman near him, but he decided that Indian gal is all right."

That story makes me feel glad. Sally's persistence was rewarded.

"How is Sarah Hillman?" I ask, eager for any news of Chilmark.

"Do you have a fever?" Ezra Brewer signs comically. "Since when does that haughty chit deserve your consideration?"

"She's not that bad," I insist, all things considered.

"How about Reverend Lee?" I ask.

"Aye, he feels right sorry," Ezra Brewer signs, "for bringing that villain into town under his protection."

"It's not his fault," I insist.

"I know it," he signs. "But like all good Christians, his conscience troubles him."

As we continue our voyage, we pass the remnants of a boat.

"A wrecked whaler," Ezra Brewer signs, removing his cap.

"What happened?" I ask.

"What usually does," he replies. "Whaling boats are sunk by injured whales trying to escape the harpoon. In some cases, the whale crashes its head into the hull of the boat, smashing it to splinters and causing it to sink with the terrified whalers struggling for their lives on the open sea."

"Doesn't it hurt the whale?" I ask.

"No," he signs. "You take less damage hitting something head-on."

I shiver, thinking of the loss of life.

Ezra Brewer changes the subject. "Better check the fish hook," he signs. He heads toward the stern and brings back the catch of the day. An old friend has a small fish flapping in her mouth.

"Smithy!" I exclaim.

"Where else would she be?" Ezra Brewer asks. "She's a regular one-eyed pirate. Her treasure is of the fishy variety."

Smithy walks over to greet me, fish in mouth, her belly swinging. I stroke her thick coat while she eats her catch.

I know the rest of the journey will not be so jovial. Andrew Noble is pursuing us. I am counting on my roguish captain to vex him.

Now I need sleep.

The cabin's basin is chipped, but the mattress is fresh hay. I pick up the blanket. It is my quilt that Mama made for my tenth birthday. She must have given it to Ezra Brewer with a clean nightgown and mobcap. I hold it to my face and inhale its familiar scent as I change clothes and snuggle into bed. Smithy keeps me warm, and the sea rocks me back and forth. I tuck the map of memories under the hay for safekeeping.

Chapter Thirty-One

We've been sailing three days. I chart the *Defiance*'s progress with Ezra Brewer's spyglass. We are both tense, though he shows it less than I do. Still, I feel it in his movements, the way he watches as he alternates between tasks, checking the rigging, navigating with the deftness of an old sea hand.

Though we have a lead on Andrew Noble, he is in steady pursuit.

There is little for me to do but feel as if I am in the way. I play with Smithy for a time, but she saunters off eventually to attend to her own feline affairs.

When evening approaches, I am no longer able to spy the *Defiance* with my bare eyes. I am relieved to think that Andrew has given up.

To keep the chill of the winter ocean at bay, Ezra Brewer gives me his thick woolen socks. I pull them up like stockings above my knees. They are large and sag on my legs.

He signs, "My apologies that I have nothing fancier to match your finery."

I stick my tongue out at him and he cackles.

The sky looks so big when you are in the middle of the ocean on a boat. Tonight, there are red and pink streaks, stretching out for miles. I rub my eyes to stay awake a few more minutes.

Watching me, Ezra Brewer signs, "Red sky at night, sailor's delight."

I imagine he's speaking to more than just the weather. Let it indeed be a good omen.

I sign, "Mama once called you a privateer."

He signs, "Did she, indeed?"

I nod.

"Aye," he signs, "that was a long time ago."

"Won't you tell me?" I ask. A bedtime tale told well in signs can reignite a flame in one's soul.

He rubs his hands together.

"It was Captain Wemyss Orrock of London. That's quite a name, isn't it? His ship, the *Hariot*, regularly transported goods between London and Jamaica.

"But in March 1776, the *Hariot* was driven into

the shoals between the Vineyard and Nantucket. Captain Orrock wasn't headed to Jamaica, though; he was carrying a load of provisions to British troops in Boston.

"He ran aground, managed to get free, but then had to anchor in safe water to wait for the currents to be in his favor. While he sat, word got back to Edgartown."

Ezra Brewer continues, quite animated. "We went out armed, in a sloop and other small boats, and demanded that Captain Orrock surrender his vessel."

"His Majesty's ship?" I ask, incredulous.

"More or less," Ezra Brewer signs, with a rueful smile. "Shots were fired, and the captain was wounded. We took him and the *Hariot* into Edgartown Harbor as a prize of war!

"Eventually, we released Captain Orrock. We weren't cutthroats, you know? In proper apparel, mind you. Some would tell you we stranded him without his breeches. That would be most improper, even for a band of mutineers."

I give Ezra Brewer a sidelong glance at that last statement.

He concludes, "We weren't commissioned, so the

profit was divided among us. I can tell you it wasn't small. The ship was taken on to Dartmouth. Whether Captain Orrock returned to England I do not know. I like to imagine him fat and happy in his ancestral home."

"Was privateering legal at that time?" I ask.

"Not exactly," Ezra Brewer admits. "The law had not yet been passed and letters of marque, or authority, were not yet being issued. Privateering was done in the name of piracy and patriotism. It wound up being an asset in the War for Independence."

"Do you feel guilty about what you did?" I ask.

"Not really," he signs, brushing cat hair off his trousers.

"You are a genuine scoundrel, sir," I observe.

"You have it," he signs.

Ezra Brewer makes the sign for walking downstairs with his fingers, and then pretends to fluff a pillow under his head.

I smile and nod. I follow Smithy down the wooden steps to the bunk.

My mind is filled with images of privateers searching for treasure. Finally, I drift off, like a baby in her mother's arms.

Chapter Thirty-Two

The next two days and night pass much the same. I assist Ezra Brewer in small ways. He gives me modest tasks to keep me occupied, like rolling the slack rope for the rigging, or searching belowdecks for any leaks or pooling water.

When I wake on the sixth day, I feel the roughness of the waters around the cutter. We are being tossed, rather than rocked. A whale oil lamp swings from a beam on the ceiling. I climb the stairs to the deck. The sea spray from large, foamy white waves makes it feel like it is raining. It numbs my face.

Ezra Brewer is still at the helm in his sealskin coat and Monmouth cap. He nods at me and smiles.

To my horror, in the distance, I spot the *Defiance*. I point, and Ezra Brewer nods, barely perceptibly. Is he not intimidated, or does he not want to show me he is alarmed?

How did Andrew catch up to us? What if he

overtakes the *Black Dog* and throws Ezra Brewer overboard? A shiver passes through me.

Ezra Brewer slips a rope anchored to the deck around the wheel to keep us on a steady course. He motions for me to come and hold the wheel, just to be certain. I think he is trying to keep my mind off what may come to pass.

While my hand holds fast to the wooden peg on the wheel, Ezra Brewer reefs the mainsail, rolling the edge of the canvas in on itself, and ties it tightly. He changes the smaller sail out for a "storm jib." He spells these words with his fingers, explaining it to me.

"We must keep the waves at the helm," he tells me, pointing behind us.

When he no longer needs my help, I fetch us hard biscuits and dried fish from the larder down below. Moving about keeps the frostbite off me. I ladle grog from a barrel for us to drink. Ezra Brewer must agree with Miss Hammond's theory that this light spirit is healthier than water.

Ezra Brewer looks tired. I've noticed him nap at the helm, then come to with a shiver and a shake of his head.

"Soon we will come close to the tip of the Cape," he signs, slipping off the sealskin coat and placing it on me. I am grateful for its warmth.

The ship rocks back and forth in the gusting winds. I stagger to keep from falling. The rain turns to hail. Small white stones pelt us and gather in piles on deck. I scoop them up and throw them overboard before the waves rush over the sides and melt them into blocks that will slide across the deck.

I can no longer see Andrew following us. Did he capsize?

The waves rise higher and higher, and the *Black Dog* with them. Up and down we go, cresting each one and falling back down, only to rise on another. My stomach turns over a few times.

In English folklore, a black dog can bring bad luck. Ezra Brewer is rascally and named his boat after a dark omen. "By facing the worst," he once told me, "I can only have good luck." With a black cat and a woman on board his boat, he is almost courting bad luck!

Up and down, up and down. It's like riding a wild horse over hills and jumping stone walls. How long will it go on?

Lightning strikes at regular intervals as if it is right above my head. I can feel a crack in the sky, and the strange hum of electricity that follows. During one great flash, I see the *Defiance* is beside us! It sideswipes the *Black Dog*. Where did it come from?

"Go below!" Ezra Brewer signs one-handed, gripping the wheel.

I don't want to leave him. I crouch down on the deck, to keep out of the way.

Another boom of thunder and zigzag of lightning. The *Defiance*, lit by the flash, goes hard to port, away from us, and circles back around. Andrew is a deft sailor, I will give him that. He uses the waves, even as they tug and toss and he struggles against the storm. The bowsprit ducks in the water as he rolls forward toward us, and I am reminded of a ram lowering its head, ready to charge.

I think of the whaler we saw and realize that Andrew intends to ram us!

I fall to the bottom of the boat and grab for the railing, afraid to be knocked over the side into the crushing sea. My captain handles the wheel rapidly, teeth gritted, and turns the boat hard. Andrew smashes alongside us again. I slide across the deck.

Suddenly, a knot slips loose in the riggings, and I lunge for it, holding on with all my might. It burns as it slips through my wet hands. I brace my feet against the slippery deck. Ezra Brewer gestures frantically for me to hold on. I wrap the rope around my wrist and tug hard.

I pray to God in Heaven to deliver us to dry land the way Noah, his family, and all the pairs of animals were delivered. Send us a dove with an olive branch to show us that we are near.

The sea is churning. Waves higher than the sides of the *Dog* flood the deck again and again.

A great wave rises out of the ocean like a pride of leaping lions and slams into the *Defiance*. I watch the schooner slowly topple in the violent sea and gasp in horror when a flash of lightning illuminates Andrew's slim figure trying to keep hold of the sinking ship. The way the waves are battering it, there seems no chance for it to right itself.

It appears suspended in its strange, lopsided position. I hold my breath and watch another wave hit. It turns turtle, the barnacled bottom facing upward, the mast pointed downward to the seabed. Do I see a hand reach out of the roiling ocean, then disappear?

We are fighting the storm too hard to help. Ezra Brewer must have struck a bargain with the sea god Neptune because he somehow keeps the *Dog* afloat.

When at last the storm starts to abate, I slump onto the deck. The pooled water soaks my skirts down to my wiry legs. I shake with cold but am too exhausted to go below. Ezra Brewer comes over and helps me pry my frozen fingers from the rope I've been clutching.

I see him shake his head and then suck his teeth. He tells me to wait and goes belowdecks to retrieve a salve for my wounds and scraps of cloth for bandages. My palms look as if they have been burned in the shape of the rope; my knuckles are crooked knots. He massages my hands gently, bringing feeling back into them.

As he works, he nods to a tune inside his own head. A shanty no doubt.

"Your hands are rougher than they were before," he observes.

I nod. I must look sad because he chucks a finger under my chin. "Maybe now you'll learn those knots, eh?

So's next time you're in a storm, you'll just tie off a rope instead of holding on to it through the whole blasted thing!" he teases, and it makes me smile.

We sit together and share mugs of grog as rays of thin sunshine begin to peek between the clouds. Ezra Brewer looks whipped by a thousand storms.

"No wreckage of the SS *Defiance*," I observe. My signing is a little awkward on account of my sore hands and bandages.

"Nay," he signs, "too much time has passed, and the waves have carried us too far. Try not to think on it. The good reverend will get word back to his family in Connecticut. You and your own have borne enough."

Somehow Ezra Brewer's words help me see that when Mama, Papa, and I were left to cope with George's loss, we pulled apart instead of coming together. I won't let that happen again.

The seas are calm for now. My mind is clearer than it has been in a long time, maybe ever. I point to the stairs, signaling Ezra Brewer to go rest. He nods and smiles before making his way belowdecks to check for damage. And then to his bunk, for a well-deserved nap.

236

Is this truly the end of my ordeal?

I stand close to the rail and survey the ocean around me. There isn't another boat in sight. The waves have calmed to ripples, and there is something so hopeful about full sails. But my sorrow needs a release. I sit sobbing, without wiping my face, until all my tears have been shed. I'm glad Ezra Brewer doesn't see me.

Chapter Thirty-Three

As soon as Ezra Brewer has taken his rest, we are on our way again. I am increasingly anxious about returning home.

"Why did you assist Andrew with the genealogy?" I ask.

"You mean those scribbles I wrote down about the Lamberts and Skiffes?" he signs.

"You mean you lied?" I ask

"Of course not, I am a man of my word," he signs, pretending to be annoyed by my accusation.

"But . . . ," I sign, encouraging him to tell me the whole truth.

Ezra Brewer scratches his chin, and the corners of his mouth form a puckish smile.

"It is true," he signs, "that your father's second cousin was deaf as a post. But it is not as well-known that her nickname was Pattycake, if it even was."

I erupt with laughter. "Pattycake? Pattycake Lambert? That's what you wrote?"

"I did indeed," he signs. "And that Yalie, with his clever ways, couldn't tell when he was being fooled."

"He wasn't clever," I sign soberly.

"I know it," he signs. "Honestly, Mary, if I had known what that man had in mind to do to you, I would have chased him back to his schooner the day he arrived."

There's something I have to get off my chest before we arrive home.

"It is different in Boston," I tell Ezra Brewer. "They don't sign. They look down on us, like we're animals."

"I've been there," he signs. "Watched all their lips flapping, and I don't believe they are a wick smarter than Vineyard folk. Take you. I've been watching you for all your years. You've got something in you, girlie."

"Some people don't think that's good," I sign.

"Pay them no mind," he signs. "I never do."

Since I have never taken a faraway trip off-island, I have never approached my home as an outsider from this distance. It looks small.

As we come near the shore, I stand on the bow of the *Black Dog*, peering through the spyglass. Matthew

Pye is gazing back. Standing on a hill, he signs "welcome" by bringing his arms down from above his head to the middle of his chest. I am warmed by the gesture.

Then I see him jump on his horse and ride off. He must be spreading the news of our return.

Will Mama and Papa be on the beach when we dock? I hope Nancy comes too.

The hills and the beach look the same. A familiar collection of boats is scattered on the shore, with men I've known all my life hauling nets out of the sea. I can even see the bottom of our sheep farm. The sheep are like squiggles of paint on a winter landscape. Snow covers some of the ground. There are patches of brown turf and thickets of bare oak and fruit trees. The pitch pines have not dropped all their needles.

Ezra Brewer slowly steers us toward the beach. He marches the bow till the water is knee-deep. Then he turns it seaward and tosses the anchor. Fishermen walk through the icy water in their winter gear to pull the cutter safely onto the sandbar.

I stand still, cold and bruised, my hair wildly blowing like a mermaid's and my cheeks sunburned. I face the shore, wearing Ezra Brewer's sealskin coat with the map of memories tucked safely inside a pocket. I hold on to Smithy until she struggles and leaps to shore.

Before Ezra Brewer and the men unload his gear, Papa comes for me.

"Mary," he signs, brushing his hand tenderly across his cheek. "Thank the Lord you are home!"

He is better than Ezra Brewer at concealing his shock at my poor condition. He breaks into a smile, swiping the back of one big hand across his eyes. He lifts me in his strong arms and squeezes. I melt against him.

As he carries me to the beach, I see that a small crowd has gathered. But where is Mama?

I see her running! Wiping her shining blue eyes with a handkerchief. And reaching—reaching for me, arms outstretched. Then she is enfolding me in her embrace. When she touches the side of my head, I wince. Mama's hands rise to her throat, shaking. Her lips tremble, but she manages a smile.

"Really you?" she signs. "Are you okay?"

"Me," I sign. "I am better now."

Papa puts me down on the sand, retrieves a blanket

from the oxcart, and returns Ezra Brewer's sealskin coat—his only coat.

Mama's embrace is soft as velvet. I never noticed her scent before I was taken off the island. It's a combination of rose water, clean wool, and cinnamon. I run my fingers over the fine features of her face and touch her hair. I feel a gentle peal of laughter.

Mr. Pye and Miss Hammond approach us and sign, "Welcome home." It's reassuring to see their friendly faces. I smile and tell them it is good to be back.

Mama and I walk the beach to the high road, with the blanket covering my storm-beaten garments. Nancy races to greet me. She looks me up and down, the way a dog might sniff a familiar bone that went missing. She looks into my eyes.

I sign to her, "I just want to say—"

"Oh, forget it, Mary," she signs. "I have been thinking about all the ways I could have been a better friend. Don't you dare outshine me and apologize first!"

"I have a lot to tell you one day," I sign.

"I have something to tell you too," she signs as we walk.

242

Reverend Lee greets me at the high road. "My child," he signs, overcome with emotion and struggling to find the right words in his hands. "May we be able to distinguish between the angels and demons. And may you stay safe, in the bosom of your family and community for all your days."

I take the hand he offers me and smile up at him.

As Mama, Papa, and I climb on the oxcart, I look back at the ocean receding under a burnt orange sunset. It is good to be back on my island.

Chapter Thirty-Four

As we near the farm, I see Thomas and Eamon fixing the stone wall. The frozen groundswell must have upended the stones. When we pass, they stop working, take off their caps, and wave at me. I wave back and smile.

Walking through our front door, I am overcome and my knees nearly buckle. Here there are no locked doors. No labor until my hands and knees are raw. No eating from discarded plates. No being poked and prodded. This is the place where we loved and laughed. And where we grieved and fought. This is a home.

Papa lifts me and carries me to the kitchen. I feel big in his arms. Have I grown that much during my captivity? Or have I just become more conscious of my size and age?

Papa sets me down in his chair by the fire. Mama touches my fine dress, now dirty and ripped. What does she imagine?

"Bath, then tea," she signs.

While Papa drags out the wooden tub and Mama heats water in the kettle, I look toward George's bedroom. The door is open, and from a distance, it looks just as he left it.

Papa exits while I bathe. I feel no shyness stepping out of my clothes in front of Mama, though I wish to shield her eyes from my injuries and gaunt ribs. I use whale oil soap scented with lavender while Mama gently works out the knots in my hair with a baleen brush. She puts a soothing balm on my ears and hands.

At the table, I sip strong English tea with cream. Images from my time in Boston flash through my mind. It's hard to shoo them away. They are part of me now as well.

Papa opens and closes the front door. Sam comes running toward me and jumps into my lap, his paws leaving marks on my shawl and clean shift. But I don't mind. He licks my face and sneezes. I ease him onto the floor and sit beside him. Grabbing hold of his scruff, I bury my face in his softness and cry.

Mama sits beside me and rubs my back. Papa taps his pipe. After a time, I climb into my chair.

"Thank the Lord for bringing our Mary home," Mama signs.

"And thank our dear friend who twice braved the icy, perilous Cape and brought our daughter safely home to us," Papa adds.

"Amen," Mama signs.

I never thought I'd see the day when Mama said "amen" for Ezra Brewer.

She serves my favorite cranberry muffins. I take a large bite, savoring the tartness of the fruit. But my stomach grumbles and aches. Too much grog, not to mention the contents of Ezra Brewer's larder, has temporarily stifled my appetite.

"Bed," Papa signs, putting his hands beneath his tilted head. He winks at Mama.

As I walk out of the kitchen toward the stairs, Mama places her hands on my shoulders. She turns me around and leads me to George's bedroom. His bedstead and bureau have been polished. New curtains drape the windows, and a new blanket covers the bed. The small desk where he worked has been cleared of his books and papers and replaced with blank rag paper, a quill pen, and an inkwell.

246

"For me?" I ask, disbelieving.

"Miss Hammond says you have a rare talent and the makings of a fine schoolteacher," Mama signs. "I expect you will find an excellent use for her generous gifts."

My heart swells.

Still, I cannot rest easy in this bed until we clear the air.

"The things I saw you say my last night at home," I blurt out.

"I never should have said," she replies. "Honestly, Mary. I didn't mean it. I didn't even know what I was saying. I thought I had lost everything that mattered to me. A cruel lesson taught me nothing could be further from the truth."

"I want to be a good daughter," I sign.

"You are," Mama signs. She nods as her eyes fill with tears, and she takes my hands.

I look out the window. The snow and ice will thaw in a few months. Will the horrors I experienced melt away too?

Mama signs, "Sleep close by. No one can harm you." Did she sense my thoughts?

I hug her for a long time before I kneel on the red braided rug next to my bed. I give thanks to Our Lord and Ezra Brewer for bringing me safely home, and to Mama and Papa for seeing the best in me. I add Mr. Squints, Dr. Minot, Nora, and the man in the Monmouth cap to the list of people I name in my prayers.

I also remember Andrew. "For it is in giving that we receive, it is in pardoning that we are pardoned, and it is in dying that we are born to eternal life."

I place George's map of memories safely on the desk before I slip into bed.

I want to stay awake to feel the vibrations of Mama and Papa in the bedroom next door. But I drop into a sound sleep.

Chapter Thirty-Five

When I rise, I put on the dress Mama made for my Christmas present. It is still folded and tied with a velvet bow. It has a floral pattern with pink and green roses embroidered on a cream-colored wool gown. A gold coin is sewn into the hem for luck.

There are two roses on my new petticoat, which no one will see but me. They are like a secret between Mama and me. I put on new woven stockings and an old pair of brown shoes.

Mama is in the kitchen. Her face lights like the sun when she sees me. She rushes about as if I am a special guest.

After a scrumptious breakfast of johnnycakes with syrup, Mama signs, "Get your cloak," and smiles. Happy little wrinkles beside her eyes appear, something I have not seen in a long time.

When I am tucked into my cloak and hat, she takes my hand and leads me outside along the high road through the remnants of snow. I wonder where we are going.

We see Mrs. Tilton and Carrie in the lane. Carrie embraces me. Mama pauses to speak with Mrs. Tilton. She is being sociable, and it makes my heart glad.

As we pass the parsonage, Mr. Lee is chipping the ice from his porch. He stops and waves to us, a gesture Mama returns warmly. We follow a wrought-iron fence farther on.

The grave markers are crooked gray landmarks among the patchy snow. She takes me to George's, which is not yet worn from the passing of time. From her cloak, she removes a Christmas wreath and hands it to me.

"You, place," she signs.

I kneel and carefully lay the wreath over his resting place while I sign the Lord's Prayer.

Then I sign, "My dear brother, I will grow up. You will always stay fifteen. Mama tells me that mockingbirds change their tune, but you cannot change your song. Is it fine to follow my own dream, if I honor all that was you and the time we spent together? We must move ahead, never forgetting, but embracing the tangible world. And loving each other more than ever."

Mama offers me her hand and helps me stand. As we walk toward home, we are at peace together for the first time in a long time.

Back in the kitchen, I smile at Mama and get to work. Without being asked, I sweep and dust. I go out to the well and carry in water to boil. I cut up the "three sisters" without complaint. I add some dried herbs to the stock in the kettle. I even clean Mama and Papa's chamber pots. Mama could not look more surprised if there were a buffalo running wild through the kitchen!

I like working side by side with Mama. The quiet rhythm of these chores feels newly satisfying. In a few months, it will be time for our big spring cleaning. I intend to help Mama with the heavy work—scrubbing, washing, and beating the rugs.

Mama taps me on the shoulder. I turn around and she signs, "Go out for your walk. I appreciate your help. You wouldn't be you if you stayed inside with me all day."

I promise Mama I will be back in a couple of hours,

to help her prepare for dinner, and I don't cross my fingers behind my back.

I pick up a fallen birch stick and walk toward the farm. I trace the tracks from a recently shod horse. I poke at an empty silver-blue mussel shell. I draw a cross on the ground where George passed on. It will always be a sacred patch of road, but his spirit has flown to Heaven.

I spot Papa and Eamon talking in the distant pastures and find Thomas in the barn. He is wrapping his possessions in a calico cloth. Is he returning home at midday? Perhaps there is an urgency in Aquinnah.

"Good morrow," I sign.

"Good to see you," he signs, with a simple gesture.

"Sally here?" I sign.

He turns around and calls to her.

To my happy surprise, she walks toward us with her mama. They must all be riding home together. Perhaps there is a Wampanoag ceremony. Papa does not prevent Thomas from observing his traditions. But I am surprised that the Skiffes let Helen and Sally off early.

"We're glad to have you back, Mary," Helen signs

warmly. She takes my hands in hers. When we let go, she has placed a necklace in my hand. I recognize the white wampum beads made from whelk shells and the carved green serpentine found in rocks and named for its snakelike hue. Both of these are used in gift exchange, and Helen must have chosen the colors and textures especially for me.

I touch my heart and sign, "Thank you."

Helen signs, "You're welcome. Stay safe. Be well."

I turn to Sally and sign, "I heard you helped Bayard. Thank you. George would have been grateful. Were you able to bring your horses from Aquinnah to teach him how to be a good horse?"

"No," she signs. "Your papa thought his neighbors might consider the presence of our horses and men a threat to your town."

"Sorry," I sign, looking downward.

"It's all right," she signs with a smile. "Your father is allowing me to take him to Aquinnah, since he likes me best of all."

I think George would approve. He'd want his horse well cared for. I'm not sorry to see him go to a good home.

I sign, "But how did you know the ways to heal Bayard?"

"Just good sense," she signs. "Poultices and good sense."

"Horse sense," Thomas teases, pulling his hand behind his head to indicate a mane.

Sally shakes her head with a smile.

"Though I like the horses best, I am caring for our animals in Aquinnah too," she signs. "Papa is teaching me what he learned on your farm, and Mama shows me remedies for their ailments."

Papa comes up behind me. We walk the Richards family, now including Bayard, to the high road. Papa shakes Thomas's hand, bows to Helen, and pats Sally on the head. I sign, "Fare thee well."

As we turn away, I ask, "Thomas will return for the big shearing in March?"

"Perhaps." Papa weighs the possibility in his hands. "He is considering going off to sea on a whaler."

"That's dangerous work," I sign, remembering the wrecked whaler I saw with Ezra Brewer.

"It is an opportunity for him to greater provide for his family," he explains. "He'd prefer if Helen and Sally didn't have to labor in homes like the Skiffes'. It's more than whales he has to worry about. Even though he is a freedman, he runs the risk of being captured and sold into slavery. And then there's the question of whether the English captain will pay his Wampanoag crew what he promised."

I must look distraught.

Papa signs, "Still, the Wampanoag of Gay Head are skilled whalers. I shouldn't be surprised if we see Thomas Richards again."

"Good," I sign, slapping the back of one hand into the palm of the other.

Papa walks toward the house with me. I think there is a part of him that is afraid to let me out of his sight.

"Papa," I ask, "what should I do when Nancy and her parents speak badly about freedmen and the Wampanoag and treat them unkindly? It's not right. It's not fair to treat people as less because they are different. Even Mama has said things that make me blush."

"Mary," Papa signs, "you are a good daughter. But you have told lies and spoken with prejudice too. It's best not to judge others. First look inside yourself. Make yourself the best person you can be. People will be influenced by your example.

"Look at my great-grandpa Lambert," Papa continues. "If it were not for him, we would not be here in the New World. Because of him, we live in a community where being deaf doesn't hinder us from living a full life. People were influenced by his example."

"Yes, but our New World is someone's old world, isn't it, Papa?" I sign. "The Wampanoag have lived here for a very long time. What about them? Look how they were affected by Grandpa Lambert's ways."

"That's true. He was not a perfect man. You're old enough to know that he once worked on a slave ship."

"Oh no!" I sign.

"I'm afraid so," Papa signs. "We can't hide from our ancestors' misdeeds."

I interrupt, "But we can make our own choices now."

Papa nods.

I stand a bit straighter, smile at Papa, and take his hand. While we walk, I let his words settle. "People will be influenced by your example."

256

Chapter Thirty-Six

Mama greets us at the door. I think it will take both my parents some time to trust that I am truly home.

Mama and I walk back to the kitchen while Papa returns to the farm. I show her the necklace Helen gave me.

"Did you thank her?" Mama asks, examining it in the light of the window.

I nod.

"Serpentine brings out your eyes," she signs, making sparks in front of her eyes. "You may wear it."

My smile turns to a frown when she adds, "But not to church." I will try to be an example and influence Mama in the future.

"Something smells sweet," I sign, closing my eyes and lifting my nose to smell the rich cooking aroma.

"A few friends come to visit," Mama signs. "Everyone anxious see you. We have a little celebration in your honor."

"Help?" I ask her.

She shakes her head. "Go room and rest a little."

At my desk, I smooth out the map of memories. It has had a long journey. New smudges and wrinkles adorn it. I consider that my world exists far beyond the map now.

I lie down for a spell until I feel the vibrations from activity in the kitchen. Our house is alive again, and I take a moment to enjoy it. I twist my hair back, put on my necklace, and go to greet my guests.

Papa is at the door, inviting in Miss Hammond and Mr. Pye. They've brought Nancy. She and I embrace, and I take her by the hand and lead her to my new bedroom.

She looks stricken to be in George's room, until I point out the new blanket and curtains. She walks over to the desk. "You can write now, Mary. Whatever fanciful stories come into your head."

"Oh, I don't know," I sign. "My old stories seem too frivolous now. I will have to find another, more important subject."

"I'm sure you will," she signs. "And I have my own path to pursue."

"What do you mean?" I ask.

She hesitates, then signs, "Uncle Jeremiah visited the island for Christmas. He stopped to talk to your papa. Your mama wouldn't meet him. He knows he did wrong by fleeing the way he did. He was hurt by the accident too. Not in body, but in mind and spirit. He wants to make restitution, perhaps with a college scholarship in George's name."

She reads my uncertain expression and continues signing. "He has offered to take me to live with him in Boston. He has promised to pay for music lessons and to take me to Concert Hall in Boston!"

"I am happy," I tell her. I can let go of my anger toward Jeremiah Skiffe. He is freeing Nancy from her choleric father's influence, though I'm certain her mother will miss her. It hurts to think of another boy going to college in George's stead, but it is a kind gesture.

"I am happy too," Nancy signs.

I go to greet my other guests, leaving Nancy behind to examine the map of memories.

I notice Miss Hammond is wearing a golden poesy ring, and Mr. Pye proudly tells me that he made it for her. I am impressed! It is delicate work to make such fine jewelry. It was obviously made with great love and care.

"Beautiful," I sign.

"I like your new necklace too," she signs. "You have a gift for bringing people together."

When Ezra Brewer arrives, I think she is right. Papa grins broadly as he shakes my rescuer's hand. Mama raises her eyebrows a little bit, but she seems content and even offers to take Ezra Brewer's sealskin coat.

"Aye," he signs, grinning like a rogue. His other hand is poised under the coat, and when it is removed, I see why. Underneath is a tiny kitten, mostly black but with patches of white and pumpkin-orange fur, and a yellow flank. This must have been the source of Smithy's recent rotundity. The kitten is tiny. "I've saved ye the runt of the litter, Mary," he tells me with a wink. "I call her Yellow Leg."

I turn to Mama. "May I keep the kitten?" I plead.

"Your father and I have already agreed to it, as soon as she's weaned from her mother," she signs. "We'll see what Sam has to say about it."

260

I almost kiss Ezra Brewer but think better of it. "Thank you!" I sign.

Mama is signing to all, "Come in, come in."

We sit around the table. Yellow Leg is tucked into my lap.

There aren't fresh flowers yet, but Mama has laid out the daintiest dishes from the cupboard. We wave our hands in applause when she sets the pudding on the table. It is made from suet and treacle with delightful candied orange slices. Mama knows I always look forward to her Christmas pudding. This more than makes up for the one I missed.

Mama pours ale for the men and Miss Hammond. Papa slips me a quick sip. No interpreter is needed. We eat in contented silence, searching one another's faces, making amusing expressions while our hands are full, and laughing together while we ask for seconds and empty our plates. It is a relief to be home.

Afterward, we move to the sitting room. Mama and Papa sit on one sofa, with Miss Hammond and Mr. Pye on the other. Ezra Brewer sits in the rocking chair in the corner, with Nancy, Yellow Leg, and I comfortable on the braided rug. The conversation is lively and civil. I hope I'll never be as suspicious of outsiders as Ezra Brewer, but Andrew sowed such discontent.

Though Ezra Brewer isn't used to playing second fiddle, he's on his best behavior with Mama as his hostess. And his latest thrilling tale is all too familiar to me. I have no desire to relive it. Tonight, Miss Hammond has a story to tell.

"In your absence, Mary," she signs, "my brother-in-law Daniel visited to trade for wool and baleen. As you know, I always ask for details of his travels to share with my students."

"You are not going to talk about mermaids and other imaginary sea creatures, are you?" Ezra Brewer asks.

"No, Ezra, I won't tell wild stories like you do," she says, giving me a wink.

Miss Hammond stands up and moves her feet like she is walking in place. She is trying to set a visual scene for her audience. It's not too different from what she does in the classroom.

She begins, "After a long journey, Daniel was glad

to have his feet planted firmly on the ground again in Paris, France. Out walking, a Frenchman in front of him was gesturing animatedly to his companion, and his companion was answering in a similar pattern. Daniel recognized the rhythm of language, so he rushed to catch up with the men. They were talking in signs!"

"Were their signs like ours?" I blurt out, my hands moving fast.

"No," Miss Hammond signs. "That's what confused Daniel. Their movements were different from anything he'd seen on the Vineyard. They spelled their names for him. Daniel couldn't decipher it at first. It seems that the French make the manual alphabet with one hand!"

Miss Hammond continues. "Daniel followed the men. He discovered that they live at a grand school for young deaf people. As a matter of fact, one of them was a teacher."

Ezra Brewer rocks back and forth and signs, "I ought to be getting to bed." He fluffs an imaginary pillow under his head and yawns theatrically.

"Please stay, Ezra," Miss Hammond encourages him like an unruly pupil. "The best is yet to come."

Ezra Brewer crosses his arms and waits.

Miss Hammond signs, "At the deaf school, Daniel saw dozens of people walking down every path and hallway signing together. They must have come from all over the country.

"There was a big room with seats in a circle like a theater. Deaf men, older pupils, and teachers stood up front and gave lectures in sign to the general public to demonstrate the success of the school and the faculties of deaf-mutes. They were smartly dressed and dazzled the audience.

"From Daniel's description, I dare say one or two of them were more colorful than Ezra in their signing." Miss Hammond glances coyly at Ezra Brewer.

He uncrosses his arms and signs, "Harrumph." He makes a fancy movement with his left hand to indicate French people. Like many Americans, he considers himself superior to Frenchmen.

She starts signing again. "One gentleman named Laurent really impressed Daniel. It wasn't just his signs, but his facial expressions. He performed famous scenes in history—like the storming of the Bastille during the French Revolution—with a few hand signs and a lit-up face that showed every emotion. Visitors who knew no sign language could guess what he was talking about."

After what I learned in Boston, the idea that a school attracts the deaf from all over their country, possibly all over the world, and gathers them for education is astounding. To think of all those deaf people, with stories so very different from mine, gathered in one place. I feel greedy to share in their stories, and to tell mine!

Miss Hammond signs, "In all Daniel's travels, he says our island and the school in Paris are the only two places he's seen sign language. He's visited places where one family has created simple hand signs to communicate with a deaf relative in the home, but no other places where everyone speaks the same signs.

"Though I've read that the Plains Indian Nations, like Crow and Cheyenne, use a complex sign language," she adds. "Not just for trading between tribes, but for storytelling and everyday conversation too. I understand most of them are not deaf."

"True?" I ask Papa.

"I suppose so," Papa says.

Miss Hammond signs, smiling, "On my honor as a schoolteacher."

I turn to Mama and ask, "You think we will have a deaf school in America soon?"

"I expect so," she replies.

"If children go there from the Vineyard, will they forget island sign language?" I wonder.

Papa signs, "I don't imagine that will happen."

I can't hear Grandmother Harmony's clock on the mantelpiece, but I see that it is growing late. Mama rises, signaling to everyone.

Mr. Pye and Miss Hammond leave together. They offer Ezra Brewer a ride, but he'd rather walk. "Don't worry about me," he signs, tucking Yellow Leg back under his coat. "I'll follow the stars."

Papa will drive Nancy home. He taps me on the shoulder. I turn around to face them both.

"Bid farewell to your friend," he tells me. "She'll be leaving first thing in the morning."

I hold up my hand to indicate that I will return quickly. I run to the desk in my room. I bring out the map of memories and place it in her hands.

"Don't forget!" I sign broadly as Papa drives her away.

"Never!" she signs, looking back. Then she's gone.

I realize too late I forgot to ask her the whereabouts of Grandmother Edith's teapot. But I expect her to return to the Vineyard one day. None of us can stay away forever.

Chapter Thirty-Seven

Before I climb into bed, I peer into the looking glass and try to tell the story of the Boston Massacre with only my face. My eyes just look wild, my expression comical. The Frenchman Miss Hammond described must be a magician.

Lying under my new blanket, my mind is full of ideas.

I feel hopeful that men like Laurent will come to America with their Paris sign language. If people in Boston and the other colonies see them as teachers and great thinkers, maybe they won't disparage the deaf anymore. If I changed Dr. Minot's mind about the deaf, imagine what deaf scholars could do.

But what will that mean for our close-knit community in Chilmark?

It's late. I yawn and snuggle under my blanket. As I do, a bedtime story comes . . .

Once upon a time, I travel across the land at incredible speed, day and night, through cold and heat.

I can't see where I'm going, but the place is familiar when I get there.

There are people signing. I recognize some of the signs; others I cannot easily decipher. At first, it's a confusing babble of hands. Then we begin to teach one another.

Our signs blend together to make one sign language. We keep what is unique to the places we came from. We light a beacon.

Deaf children, who can't communicate with their families and believe there is no one else like them, find us. We accept them, no matter where they come from. We take them in, even if they are angry or hurt.

I see myself in a tall stone building, looking out the window in a classroom. A stone bench in a courtyard is covered with autumn leaves and then powdery snow and then dogwood flowers. I am a student in a deaf school, and then I am a teacher.

My hair fades and ages, like the leaves in a book. Others take my place and write their own stories. They read the book I wrote and say, "That's how it was on their island. It is different now. But they came before. They helped us to become who we are. We won't ever forget them."

⌒ A NOTE ON THE LANGUAGES

I am Deaf. I do not speak Martha's Vineyard Sign Language (MVSL). People have tried to preserve the language, but it has never been fully documented. The last native speaker, Katie West, died in 1952.

I am a fluent speaker of American Sign Language (ASL) and because MVSL influenced the development of ASL, I have used variations of ASL signs to describe some MVSL signs. As a child, I used home signs or gestures created by my family. Those signs also influenced the sign descriptions in this book. In other words, I used the sign languages I know to create the sign language in this book.

Throughout the story, I tried to highlight the differences between sign language and spoken language. In a few scenes, I chose to show readers that sign languages have their own construction that differs from English. I wanted readers to experience a flavor of that, without distracting from the narrative. These passages are not meant to be an exact glossing, or interpretation, of modern ASL. I hope these scenes convey the intimacy, complexity, and expressiveness of sign language.

⌐HEREDITARY DEAFNESS ON MARTHA'S VINEYARD

Hereditary deafness in isolated communities is not completely unusual. These communities often created their own sign language. It is referred to as "village sign language." From 1640 through the late 1800s, hereditary deafness was common on Martha's Vineyard, especially in the town of Chilmark. At one time, one in twenty-five residents of Chilmark was born deaf. In a section of town called Squibnocket, there were as many as one in four deaf residents, compared with one in six thousand in the rest of the country.

Deafness was a recessive trait that affected White settlers equally. The genetic mutation produced complete deafness at birth with no associated anomalies.

It is true that it was brought over from the county of Kent, England, especially the region known as the Weald, by prominent families like the Lamberts, Skiffes, and Tiltons. It is believed that they also brought Old Kentish Sign Language with them. The English use a two-handed manual alphabet to this day.

Because the families in the small-knit farming and fishing village intermarried for generations, the trait for deafness remained strong. It started to disappear as residents moved off-island and married outsiders.

Because there was a complete lack of knowledge of Mendelian

genetics at the time, scientists were puzzled that families could have both deaf and hearing relatives, in a seemingly random pattern. Some of the theories of the time are described in this book: environmental factors, maternal fright, and even tight corsets during pregnancy!

The one major study on the subject is Nora Ellen Groce's ethnography: *Everyone Here Spoke Sign Language*, Harvard University Press, 1985. I could not have written this book if I hadn't read that one.

⌒DEAF EDUCATION AND AMERICAN SIGN LANGUAGE

In 1817, the American School for the Deaf opened in Hartford, Connecticut, laying the groundwork for the development of a national sign language. The school in its earliest years was a mixture of different sign languages. Some students came from village sign communities, a notable example being Martha's Vineyard. Others had created home signs that only their families understood. The American School for the Deaf was a Whites-only school, and Deaf education was largely segregated into the mid-twentieth century.

The school's cofounder and first teacher, Laurent Clerc, was a former pupil of the Paris school, the first free school for the Deaf in the world, established in 1670. He introduced Old French Sign

Language and the one-handed manual alphabet to America. Though lesser known by the general population than Thomas Gallaudet, Clerc is still greatly revered in Deaf culture.

Eventually, MVSL, home sign, and the French system merged into what would become American Sign Language (ASL).

Home sign still exists in families, as do village sign communities in many countries. There are dialects in contemporary ASL, both regional and cultural. Some vibrant examples are Black American Sign Language (BASL) and American Indian Sign Language (AISL), which is distinct from Plains Sign Talk (PISL). Each of these sign languages has its own rich traditions and history.

Every country in the world has its own sign language; some have more than one.

THE NAMING OF MARTHA'S VINEYARD

There are several versions of the story. I went with English captain Bartholomew Gosnold naming it after his baby daughter in 1602. I followed Arthur R. Railton's telling of Gosnold searching for the "happy and beautiful bay" described by Giovanni de Verrazzano in a letter to King Francis I of France. Railton's book, *The History of Martha's Vineyard: How We Got to Where We Are*, Commonwealth Editions, 2006, was helpful in many instances.

The Wampanoag Tribe of Gay Head (Aquinnah) is a federally recognized, sovereign tribe of Wampanoag people based in the town of Aquinnah ("high land") on Martha's Vineyard. Their ancestors have lived on the island of Noepe ("land amid the waters") for at least ten thousand years.

In the early 1800s, many Wampanoag men had died from diseases that settlers brought, or left the island to find work. The Wampanoag women welcomed freedmen as husbands. Their children were Wampanoag of Aquinnah.

Aquinnah Wampanoag practices of welcoming members into their tribe regardless of blood quantum, accepting mixed-race marriages and offspring, and owning land collectively were regarded as wrong by the English settlers. These differences created more prejudice and discrimination against the Wampanoag.

In 1972, the Wampanoag Tribal Council of Gay Head, Inc., was formed to promote self-determination, to ensure preservation and continuation of Wampanoag history and culture, to achieve federal recognition for the Tribe, and to seek the return of tribal lands to the Wampanoag people. The Wampanoag Tribe of Gay Head (Aquinnah) became a federally acknowledged tribe on April 10, 1987, through the Bureau of Indian Affairs (BIA).

In Herman Melville's *Moby Dick*, the stereotypical character of Tashtego is Aquinnah Wampanoag. In 1902, Amos Smalley, an Aquinnah whaler, harpooned his own great white sperm whale, the only man who has ever done so. The Tribe retains to present day their aboriginal rights to any drift whales that beach along or near the shores of Noepe.

There is a Wôpanâak Language Reclamation Project to teach Wampanoag children their language.

Two books greatly helped in my research. *Moshup's Footsteps: The Wampanoag Nation, Gay Head/Aquinnah; The People of First Light* by Helen Manning, Blue Cloud Across the Moon Publishing, 2001; and *The Wampanoag Tribe of Martha's Vineyard: Colonization to Recognition* by Thomas Dresser, The History Press, 2011. Lastly the Tribe's official webpage, wapmanoagtribe.org, is the best resource.

⁓ ACKNOWLEDGMENTS

I want to thank the following people:

Brian Selznick wrote *Wonderstruck*, an extraordinary book about Deaf culture, history, and language, and paid it forward by introducing me to his editor at Scholastic Press, Tracy Mack.

Tracy was a great partner and mentor for this book. She saw what I was trying to do before I did. I am grateful for her tough revisions, excitement for the project, and understanding that not all writers are coming to English from the same direction. Her patience and guidance are deeply appreciated, and she has uncanny instincts for what works, even beyond her cultural experiences. I am enriched by our friendship.

During Tracy's sabbatical, I worked with editor Leslie Budnick, whose friendly emails were always welcome and who left her unique mark on the story.

Assistant editor Benjamin Gartenberg was knowledgeable, insightful, and helpful from beginning to end. An essential member of the team.

I am delighted and honored to have Julie Morstad's cover art. Special thanks to art director Marijka Kostiw and production editor Melissa Schirmer.

I am grateful to my sensitivity readers. Cherryl Toney Holley, the current chief of the Hassanamisco band of the Nipmuc Nation, who is also hearing impaired, provided key historical information. Penny Gamble-Williams of Wampanoag and African heritage is an activist involved in Native land, freedom of religion and sacred site issues, and Indigenous and environmental rights. She is a member of the Chappaquiddick Tribe of the Wampanoag Nation. Her generous, in-depth assistance and enthusiasm for the project was of inestimable help. I admire her work as an artist and the museum exhibits she has created. Tom L. Humphries is an American academic, author, and lecturer on Deaf culture and deaf communication; I appreciate his input.

Thanks to the Alachua County Library District. I'm grateful for all I've learned from my colleagues, with a focus on children's literature and working with underserved communities. Special thanks to the following: Ross Woodbridge, Debbie Lewis, Sol Hirsch, Phillis Filer, Al Martin, Shannon Kitchen, Caryl McKellar, J. T. Whitfield, Jessica Jaegar, Sabrina Sturzenbecker, Tomiko Kutyna, Heather Sostrom, Jackie Seekamp, Lauren Brosnihan, Robert Fryling, Erin Phemester, Odette Hinson, Tina Bushnell, Kerry Dowd, Gabriela Sheremet, Emily Young, Linda Steffanelli, Bill Juniper, Jodie Patterson, Elaine Needelman, and Chris Culp.

Thanks to my friends in the School Board of Alachua County, Deaf/HOH specialist Tina Kercheval, ASL teacher Rachael LaCombe, and media specialists Bart Birdsall and Judith Weaver.

Special thanks to my sister-in-law, Katrina Goodrich. And to Alexis Redhorse Blendel and Sally Ford.

All gratitude and love to my sister, Jean Marie Le Zotte. She read and commented on every draft of this story, enriching it with her edits, questions, and comments. Her knowledge on many subjects, such as the will-o'-the-wisps legend and sailing ships, made her an endless resource. Her innate sympathy for how the world sometimes treats me because I'm Deaf carried me through the hardest rewrites. She is my magical witch, fellow writer, and family. Our little dog, Perkins, also makes life warmer and funnier.

I was lucky to have my parents, Bess George Le Zotte (1942–2004) and Edward Harrison Le Zotte (1935–2004). When you grow up ill and/or disabled, you need that person who sees you as whole and believes you can do anything. That was Dad.

And thanks to the cab driver who first told me about the island's Deaf history when I was living on Cape Cod in the 1990s and made my first trip to Martha's Vineyard!

⌇⌇THE TEXT OF THIS BOOK WAS SET IN 12 POINT ADOBE GARAMOND PRO, A CONTEMPORARY TYPEFACE FAMILY BASED ON THE ROMAN TYPES OF CLAUDE GARAMOND AND THE ITALIC TYPES OF ROBERT GRANJON.

⌇⌇THE TITLE TYPE AND AUTHOR NAME WERE HAND-LETTERED BY JULIE MORSTAD.

⌇⌇THE JACKET ART WAS CREATED WITH PENCIL AND DIGITALLY RENDERED BY JULIE MORSTAD.

⌇⌇THE BOOK WAS PRINTED ON NORBRITE OFFSET AND BOUND AT LSC COMMUNICATIONS.

⌇⌇PRODUCTION WAS OVERSEEN BY MELISSA SCHIRMER.

⌇⌇MANUFACTURING WAS SUPERVISED BY IRENE CHAN.

⌇⌇THE BOOK WAS DESIGNED BY MARIJKA KOSTIW AND EDITED BY TRACY MACK.